Sacred Omega

Aiden Bates
Jill Haven

© 2019

Disclaimer

All rights reserved. No part of this publication may be reproduced, distributed, or transmitted in any form or by any means, including photocopying, recording, or other electronic or mechanical methods, without the prior written permission of the publisher, except in the case of brief quotations embodied in critical reviews and certain other noncommercial uses permitted by copyright law.

This is a work of fiction. Names, places, characters and events are all fictitious for the reader's pleasure. Any similarities to real people, places, events, living or dead are all coincidental.

This book contains sexually explicit content that is intended for ADULTS ONLY (+18).

Contents

Chapter 1 4
Chapter 2 8
Chapter 3 12
Chapter 4 15
Chapter 5 20
Chapter 6 25
Chapter 7 29
Chapter 8 35
Chapter 9 39
Chapter 10 47
Chapter 11 51
Chapter 12 55
Chapter 13 58
Chapter 14 64
Chapter 15 67
Chapter 16 72
Chapter 17 76
Chapter 18 80
Chapter 19 84
Chapter 20 87
Chapter 21 91
Chapter 22 95
Chapter 23 99
Chapter 24 104
Chapter 25 108
Chapter 26 112
Chapter 27 114
Chapter 28 118
Chapter 29 122
Chapter 30 125
Epilogue 130

Chapter 1
Matthew

I pushed the pile of rejected applications around my coffee table with my heel as I patiently listened to the most recent polite, professional rejection. This one was delivered on the phone at least, which was a step up from a bland form letter. I supposed that was progress. Not really progress toward using my heinously expensive paleontology degree, or paying off the loans for it or anything. Call it progress toward getting used to the rejections.

"...is a very competitive field and there were many qualified candidates for this project," the woman said. I had already forgotten her name. Not that I didn't care, but after twenty or so of these things it was hard to keep track. "We hope that you'll apply to our next dig, and if we come across anything we feel you'd be a fit for, we'll be sure to pass your resume along. You really do have an excellent resume, Mr. Stiles."

"Thank you for that," I replied, carefully measuring my tone to be as grateful as I could be. "Of course I'm disappointed, but I appreciate the consideration. You have a good evening. Or afternoon over there, I guess, right?"

"Yes," the woman said. "You as well, Mr. Stiles."

We hung up, and I resisted the urge to hurl my phone across the room. Thirty applications. I had sent out *thirty* requests to be considered for everything from digs to restoration projects. Statistically, it seemed like I should have been accepted to a project just from the sheer number of applications. A master's degree didn't go as far these days as it did when my grandfather was alive, apparently.

Which, realistically, meant getting into a post-grad program. And another hundred thousand in student loans. Fantastic.

The door to my little two-room apartment opened, and my roommate, Yuri, bustled through the door hauling a cardboard file box. It looked enormous on his small frame and he struggled to close the door with one foot. I rushed to help him.

"Thanks," he breathed. "Midterms are in. Hooray."

"You wanted it," I reminded him. Yuri was in a grad program already, which was a little easier when you had rich Ukrainian parents who were *not* allegedly connected to Russian oligarchs. As far as anyone could prove.

"People want to drink, too," he shot back, "but they do not ask for hangovers."

He shucked his coat and tossed it on the free hook by the door, then peered at my face. "You look depressed."

"It's a new look I'm trying," I said.

I took the box of midterm papers to the living room and placed it on the coffee table beside my library of shame. Yuri looked it over with a sympathetic frown. "I take it you have had no success."

"None." I flopped onto the second-hand sofa that made up twenty-five percent of the furniture in the living room and groaned softly as I ran my fingers through my hair. "I must have pissed someone off. My references are all professors that I thought I had good relationships with but someone's got to be fucking me. You know there are twenty people on the team in Siberia digging up some old mammoth carcasses and they're getting paid about ten dollars a day? For them I was overqualified, never mind that I literally told them I would take five."

"Get your PhD," Yuri suggested as he strolled to the kitchenette by the entryway and poured us both a glass of water. He grinned as he turned back to me. "It's nonstop fun and games, I promise."

I eyed his box of papers to be graded. "It looks like it, and since I know they don't have sarcasm in the Ukraine, it must be true."

He passed me one of the two glasses, and I took a sip, giving my many rejections a forlorn look. "This was a mistake, Yuri. I should have gone for the history degree and settled for teaching high school. Why did I think chasing a stupid dream was a good idea?"

Yuri sighed, and sank onto the couch next to me. He clapped a hand on my thigh. "My friend, you must not despair like this. There is nothing to gain in revisiting the same bad thoughts, yes? You are brilliant, I have all faith in your eventual success. These? They are only small things. You are meant for big things. I know this. My great grandmother was a famous psychic, you know. She could see the future, and I am told I look just like her."

"Oh, is that how that works?" I asked, one eyebrow arched as I gave him a skeptical glance.

He withdrew his hand and tapped his temple. "I tell you, I have this gift."

His smile betrayed the joke, and my shoulders shook with silent laughter for just a moment. A small break from an otherwise shitty day. We both grew thoughtful in the quiet that followed.

Finally, Yuri grunted with the effort of sitting forward, and then tugged the box to his side of the table to take the cardboard lid off. He fished a paper out, and glanced at the title page. "Economic Effects of the Second Crusade on Twelfth-Century France," he read. He gave me a pained smile. "Care to read it with me?"

"Oh, that is tempting," I lied, "but I've got, like… something else to do. I don't know what yet but I'm pretty sure I can figure it—"

My phone buzzed, traveling a short distance over the table as it did. Then again. I picked it up and frowned at the name displayed. Professor Taylor?

Yuri waved frantically. "Answer it. I tell you I have the gift."

"Yeah, but—"

"Answer!" he hissed.

I rolled my eyes and answered the call. Not that I didn't like Professor Taylor—he had been one of my favorites back when I was in undergrad getting my bachelor of science in history. Before Rex and that whole mess over six years ago. Before Taylor had been booted from Oregon State for being… unstable. "Uh, hello?"

"Matthew?" Professor Taylor asked. "Matthew Stiles? It's Jon Taylor, you were in my—"

"I remember you, Professor," I assured him. "It's good to hear from you. What are you... What can I do for you?"

Yuri watched with tense interest, eyes wide and sparkling as if he really had predicted something. He didn't know that Taylor was a pariah these days.

"I believe," Taylor said, "it's what I can do for you. A little eoconfuciusornis told me you had finished your master's degree and that you're on the hunt for a project. One of your classmates, Patrick Pearly, is working a dig in South Africa, saw your name and gave me a call. I guess you weren't selected for their expansion team?"

I unclenched my jaw. "Uh, yeah. Yeah, that's accurate."

Fucking Pat Pearly. No wonder I hadn't gotten the position. And of *course* he'd called professor batshit crazy *dinosaur dragons were real* Taylor. Pearly hated me because I was top of Taylor's class and had turned him in for plagiarizing his final paper that year. He'd clearly recovered from the stain of it. There is no justice.

"Are you still looking for a position?" Taylor pressed, urgent like he was somehow excited to be talking with me. Which, for all I knew, he was. No credible, self-respecting paleontologist of any degree would want to be caught dead at one of Taylor's crackpot digs looking for dragons, unicorns, griffins, and other mythological creatures.

Yuri furrowed his brow, his head cocked a little to one side. Taylor's voice carried and the volume was up on my phone, probably he could hear everything. He nodded vigorously and waved me on, mouthing, "Say yes."

"I... am." I managed, and gave Yuri the *cut it out* eyes.

"Oh, wonderful," Taylor exclaimed, before walking it back. "Well, not *wonderful* per se. You were such a promising student, I am shocked there hasn't been a small war over where you end up. But, it's my boon. One man's... uh, well, at any rate. I have an offer for you."

This was what I amounted to. No discovering a new species of prehistoric lizard, no adventuring in the jungles of South America looking for the next Sparassodonta specimen. All I was good for was chasing wild stories just this side of flat-Earther crazy. Still, I owed it to the old man to at least hear him out. "That's great, Professor," I said, summoning scraps of enthusiasm. "What kind of, ah... what project?" If he was going to give me a job, potentially, assuming it was anything I wanted my name attached to, it wouldn't do to ask him what kind of crazy-ass nonsense he was hunting for.

There was amusement in his voice, and not a little bit of smugness. "I'm in Texas," he said, "just west of Catarina. I'm here with a team of about a dozen, it's a privately funded venture—lots of money has gone into this for the last three years. And Matthew—I've *found* something. But I don't have a... well, frankly I don't have a credible name with me. You don't have quite the same stigma on you that I do these days. I need someone to come down and confirm my findings. Or disprove them, of course."

And no one else will give you the time of day, I thought.

"It's two hundred thousand," he added.

I blinked, and Yuri sat bolt upright, eyebrows creeping slowly up.

"Two hundred thousand?" I asked. "What, the specimen? Is it a mammoth or—"

Taylor chuckled. "No, my boy," he said. "Two hundred thousand *dollars*. That's the pay, if you'll join me. Even if you disprove what I believe to be my findings. One year, for due diligence and to finish the dig. Salaried, of course, and if I'm right—if I've found what I believe I've found—not only will it utterly change the world but your name will be on the paper right beside mine."

And if I disproved whatever it was, I would be the guy that gave Professor Taylor the time of day. I could say goodbye to post-grad.

"Take it," Yuri hissed softly. "This is an opportunity, Matt. Take it; you have to."

Pressure from both sides made me uneasy. I don't like rash, spur-of-the-moment decisions and I'd made enough of them to know they could turn out badly even if they seem smart in the moment. This didn't even seem smart. Aside from the money.

And it was a lot of money. Enough to pay off a sizeable chunk of my loans. And if it gave me too much of a stink, I could always make a big deal about junk paleontology, get into the good graces of the academic royalty. Yes, it would make me feel gross to join the pile-on that was already on top of Professor Taylor but if he was wrong about whatever it was then didn't he deserve it for chasing nonsense and spending people's money to do it?

"So," Taylor pressed. "What do you say?"

"What is it you think you've found?" I asked.

Taylor gave a disappointed huff. "I'm afraid I can't tell you," he said. "It might bias your own observations when you get here and besides that I'm under an NDA half a foot thick. But I'll tell you this—you'll get ten thousand dollars just for coming down."

Ten thousand to fly to Texas and back? I admit, that was impossible to say no to.

I rolled my eyes at Yuri again before I closed them and took a long breath. "I suppose... all right. I'll come down. But I can't promise to stay involved, Professor. I should tell you that right at the start, I don't want to lead you on."

"Oh, my boy," Taylor said, and I could almost hear his wild grin, "believe me. This, you are going to want to see all the way through."

Chapter 2
Reece

I had begun to hate being in human skin. The rain was cold on my cheeks, and had begun to seep into my boots. The wind was cold despite being late spring, and after a month in Portland I had grown weary of both. For the tenth time that night, I turned into an alleyway and walked until I was thoroughly obscured by shadow, and allowed my fire just enough freedom to dry the inside of my clothes and warm my skin until wisps of steam curled away from me. Not so much to set my human clothing on fire.

At least it was the last night I had to be here. If Tarin couldn't produce the proof he promised me, I would leave the city and go back to the desert and my other body. And I suspected he would fail to fulfill his promise. It had been foolish to trust an oathbreaker in the first place. Anyone else, I would have ignored, oathbreaker or not.

After a moment to ensure my fire was thoroughly repressed, I returned to the street to start the process of soaking all over again. The place Tarin wanted to meet wasn't far. A human establishment, of course. All of them were here, and Tarin wasn't welcome anywhere that our people congregated in any case.

Oswald's was a *bar*. A place where humans gathered to drink tea made from yeast-water. The smell of them hit me before I even pulled the door open, and only got worse from there. I did my best to ignore it, and scanned the place both with my eyes and nose to pick out the faint scent of brimstone long dormant. Tarin raised a glass of yeast-tea at me when my eyes settled on him, and waved me over. There was a yellow folder on the tall, round table in front of him.

I gave the bar another look over again, by habit. Bad enough to entertain his wild notions; I didn't need to be seen with him by anyone who knew what they were seeing.

But we were, of course, the only two dragons in the room.

I took my coat off with a practiced shrug and hung it on the back of the tall stool opposite him, wordless as I took a seat and clasped my hands on the table before me.

"How's the cold treating you?" Tarin asked.

"I suspect it won't matter soon," I replied, and nodded at the folder. "Is this it, then? You plan to make this... visit worth my while?"

Tarin's congenial expression soured. "You spend too much time in your scales."

"And you are starting to look too human," I pointed out. There were hints of gray along behind his temples, peppering his dark hair with signs of mortal aging. Why he didn't simply shift them away was beyond me. The closer I looked, the more I noticed other small signs of mortality as well. Lines at the corners of his eyes, and deepening the look of his mouth. Gray eyes didn't quite have the shine they did when he first went mad and committed to living among mortals. "When's the last time you were among your own people?"

He snorted softly and took a long pull from his glass. It landed a bit too loudly on the table when he set it back down, the liquid sloshing almost to the edge. "I can't tell if you're trying out humor or not."

"There is a whole aerie of oathbreakers in the Rockies," I said. "It isn't as though you have no one."

"No one worth a damn," he muttered. He raked a hand through his hair and waved it off. "I'm not here to talk about all that. You wanted proof there are Templars around. Here it is."

He pushed the folder across the table to me.

I admit hesitating a fraction of a heartbeat. Templars anywhere seemed unlikely. They'd been dead for three hundred years. I'd barely been of breeding age when the last of them was finally exterminated. Still, I picked up the folder and opened it to see a series of photos. "What am I looking at, exactly?"

Tarin leaned over the table and pointed to a human male's chest in a small crowd at some kind of faire. I looked more closely, adjusting my eyes for the poor light in the room, and saw half a tattoo of some kind where his fingertip was. To be sure, it looked like one-half of the icon of the Templars. Problem was…

"So he has a tattoo," I said. "So? Their icons are not the secrets they were before the internet. I suspect that thousands, if not hundreds of thousands, of humans have their imagery inked on them. This isn't proof of anything, Tarin."

"Keep going," he said. "I followed this same man for two weeks. See for yourself."

The pictures told a story in what seemed like chronological order. The man with the tattoo met two others briefly at the faire—one of them had a tattoo in the same place, visible only briefly as the wind pushed at his collar—the other was unmarked, but they had serious expressions. A picture of the first alleged Templar getting into a black town car. Parking before an old church in Northwest. Greeting someone at the door and shaking hands.

I started to move to the next picture but Tarin stopped me. "Look at their hands."

I did. "They're shaking hands," I said flatly. "Humans do that. Surely you've seen it before? I barely spend any time—"

"That's not how people shake hands," Tarin said, clearly frustrated. "They're grabbing at the elbow, it's an old-world style and the tradition of the Templars. That plus the tattoo, plus the clandestine meeting place?"

Perhaps it was slightly compelling. But it wasn't really proof. I closed the folder and pushed it back across the table. "It could as easily be mortal enthusiasts play-acting at a secret cabal of some kind. Where would they have inherited the traditions from? Even if they called themselves Templars, that wouldn't make them dragon slayers, Tarin. It just makes them children playing pretend."

Tarin opened the folder, and took out the last three photos to lay them in front of me. "You think I don't know about humans and their penchant for secret clubs and appropriation? Look here.

They're watching someone. This young man. I thought it was him and another at first, but they only followed the dark-haired one."

It was the first man from the faire again. This time, however, he had a camera and was in the same town car as before, snapping photos of someone. The next shot was of an athletic-looking human male, dressed in jeans and a suit coat and boots. He had a satchel hanging from his shoulder. In the second picture he faced the camera as he walked. For a human, he was attractive enough.

"A dragon?" I asked.

Tarin shook his head. "No. Not a dragon."

"Then I fail to see the significance," I sighed. "If these people want to follow other humans around, that's none of our business. None of this remotely—"

"I got close to him," Tarin said. "He's not entirely human. He has a smell, one I haven't caught in a long time."

"Wolven?" I guessed, skeptical still. They were more likely to live among humans than we were, but not by much. They preferred their wilderness the way we preferred our caves, and in my case the warmth of desert sand.

"I tell you this," he said, "because you are my oldest friend, and because I believe they are targeting this man with the intent to kill him. And because law forbids me from intervening myself."

"Tell me what?" I pressed, irritated with Tarin's sense of needless drama. "Out with it, I'll not have you make a fool of me, Tarin."

Tarin glanced past me at the door, and licked his lips. "I know you won't believe this coming from me," he whispered, "but I believe he's a sacred omega. There were two bloodlines in the new world, and last we knew, one of them had migrated, and the smell is—"

I held a hand up for silence and shook my head. "Right. I'm done here, then. If you want attention, Tarin, go to the Rockies, find the other oathbreakers. You are my friend and always will be, but I'm not risking my own honor for fairy tales and conspiracies."

"No, no," Tarin said quickly, half out of his chair as I moved to leave. A hand snatched at my wrist. "I told you, I knew you wouldn't believe my word alone. I followed the man around, he and a friend of his frequent this place. They live above us. The other one just came home. If I know them—and I've been watching him for over a week now—they'll be here soon. Almost every weeknight they come down. Just wait, and see if you don't recognize the scent. This could be important, Kestr—*Reece*, sorry. Really."

I bristled at even a fraction of my draconic name. Long tradition etched into my very being made anger bubble up as a low growl that I had to rein in with an effort. I tugged my hand out of his grip. His eyes were pleading, almost panicked, no trace of apparent deception in his expression or body language—but then, I was long out of practice reading humans, and at this point Tarin was more them than us perhaps.

Still… it was a startling prospect. A sacred omega still at large in the world? I thought the bloodlines were erased by the Templars long ago, and while there were two bloodlines reported in the new world, those rumors were believed to have been discredited.

Then again, Tarin was as bound by our ancient laws as I was, oathbreaker or no. If he was, against all probability, correct and in fact he had discovered both Templars and a sacred omega, he was of course correct—intervening was out of the question. He would be forbidden from approaching the man. And indeed, if the Templars somehow were at large and knew of the existence of one of our sacred omegas extant in the world, they would doubtless seek to exterminate him. If it was all true, then it was quite serious.

If it was all true.

I righted myself in the seat, and clasped my hands again, eyeing him with open suspicion. "I will wait," I informed him. "We shall see. If you're correct about this… well, I won't speculate. Certainly, the ancients will wish to know. And we will have to arrange that the old protocols be renewed."

"Bureaucracy," Tarin spat, disgusted and waving a hand as if I'd made a foul odor. "There's no time for process and—*there*. There, at the door. Look for yourself, breathe it in. I *told you*, Reece. It's *him*."

I turned, inhaling slowly and processing everything that I could from the room as the slight, cool breeze from the street carried a fresh bouquet of sweat, yeast, hops and—

"Sun and stars," I breathed as the scent reached my nose. It was sweet, and coppery, and vaguely cinnamon and earth. Unmistakable, but it had been so long since I scented it—more than a hundred years now—that I almost doubted my senses.

The dark-haired young man had, as Tarin predicted, arrived with his blond friend in tow. The two of them crossed the open space between the tables and the bar and found barstools, and waved for drinks. They seemed in good spirits.

"Tarin, this is…" I didn't have the words.

"I'm well aware," he said, likely thinking the same thing that I was.

For two hundred years, dragonkind had believed we were at our dusk. Though we would live, individually, for a thousand more years, our females were long gone. The omegas that we had once claimed in treaty from the Wolven had been exterminated, the Wolven themselves unwilling to give us others. We were a dying race.

But perhaps not anymore.

Unless, of course, Tarin was right about the Templars as well.

Chapter 3
Matthew

"Don't look," Yuri muttered to me, which of course made me begin to turn my head to see what it was I shouldn't look at. He widened his eyes and nudged me with his knee. "I said don't look. But at your seven o'clock is a tall dark and daddy-looking gentleman that I think may want to eat you alive. I believe that you should let him."

My cheeks warmed. I gave him a playful but scolding shove. "Yuri!"

"I do not mean literally," he assured me, and bit his lip. "I mean just your ass."

I groaned and threw back the rest of my beer. "Okay, well, it's a boys' night out. I'm not planning on bringing anyone up, we're celebrating. Plus, you have work to do."

"I also have headphones." He waggled his eyebrows at me. "You have not been laid in a long time. What is the harm? He looks like he can do things... things that may be illegal in some places. And what is better than celebrating with a proper fuck?"

I barked a laugh and eyed him sideways as I pushed my glass toward the bartender and waved two fingers at him. "I'm gonna chalk that up to a language barrier issue."

"My English is better than yours." He threw back the rest of his own beer and added his glass to mine. Ever since we'd been friends, I had been drinking more. At least after three years living together I had learned to pace myself after the first one, and had convinced Yuri that vodka was not a casual kind of drink. Not at the volume he could put away. "Oh, shit. He is coming. Did you wash your ass today?"

"What?" I must have turned red. "Of course I—it doesn't matter, I'm not..."

Yuri bit his lip and turned away from me to lean on the bar, fighting a grin. I felt the presence of the man loom up behind me. Not just in the way you can tell if someone is standing there. It was almost a physical kind of warmth—as if he were pressed against me.

"Excuse me," a deep voice asked, vibrating into my bones in a way that didn't seem possible.

I turned slowly on the barstool, composing myself mentally. I had to admit, the voice was a thing. It reminded me of Rex. Which wasn't necessarily supposed to be a *good* thing. "Yes?"

He was, as Yuri assessed, tall, dark and exceedingly daddy. Not quite going gray, but with that strong, perfect jaw with just a trace of beard coming in along it, and eyes that were so intense they caught and held me fast for several moments. Handsome didn't cut it. Beautiful seemed too elegant. Refined roughness was all over the man's features, and the promise of strength filled out a dark gray suit.

I stiffened when he leaned in slightly. "I said, what's your name?"

Only at that point did I realize he'd asked me the first time. "Sorry," I muttered before I found my voice and spoke up. "Sorry—it's, ah—"

"Matthew," Yuri supplied. "His friends call him Matt."

"What he said," I confirmed. I stuck a hand out. "Matt. And you are?"

The man looked down at my hand as if considering what it was for just long enough that when he finally took it the awkwardness was real and present. His hand was hot. Not just warm—feverishly hot but not sweaty. "My name is Reece," he said.

"Hi, Reece." I extracted my hand.

"May we speak privately?" Reece asked.

I raised both eyebrows. "Uh... I'm so sorry, do I know you?"

Yuri's barely suppressed giggling nipped at the back of head but I resisted the urge to jab him.

Reece didn't seem to notice at all. His eyes were on me, at that same level of intensity that had been sexy in a scary kind of way before, but was quickly becoming unnerving the longer it went on. "No," he said. "We don't know one another. But I don't think our conversation should be in public."

Various alarms and alerts went off in different parts of my brain. Hot guy? Yes. Lonely bottom with an unsatisfied libido? Certainly. Stupid enough to just go off with a total stranger with what might well have been serial killer eyes in the middle of the night to have a conversation that 'shouldn't be had in public'? Definitely not. The bar was far from empty, at least, and there were cameras at the back corner of the room in the event of a robbery or bar fight. And the staff knew me and Yuri. As long as we were here, this was a safe place.

The math did itself quickly, and I licked dry lips as I turned slightly away to face my body toward Yuri instead of the stranger. "It's sort of a boys' night," I told Reece. "No offense. You're definitely... I appreciate the interest, it's flattering. Another night, though, I think."

Reece didn't get the message. "There may not be another night, I'm afraid. If I could speak with you alone for just a moment? I won't take much of your time, I assure you."

Yuri's giggling had subsided. He caught my eye, and then that of the bartender as our beers were delivered. He picked his up and swigged it before swirling in the chair to look Reece over head to toe. "My friend said that he is not interested. That should be enough, yes? So, if you would go?"

The bartender, Aaron, was still there, cleaning a clean glass on his side of the bar.

Reece's eyes checked Yuri, and the bartender, and then the rest of the room. He took a step back and I swear he *bowed* a little at the waist. "My apologies," he said. "I'm out of practice, it seems. I'll leave you to your yeast—to your beer, that is."

Yuri raised his glass in a mock-toast, and with that Reece withdrew. He took that strange heat with him as well, and with my nerves as on edge as they had gotten, the sensation had sort of slipped into the background. Once it was gone, I almost missed it.

"Did you feel the heat coming off that guy?" I asked Yuri as we turned back to the bar. In the bar mirror, Reece retreated to his table along the back wall, where a friend said something with considerable animation before Reece took a long coat from the chair, slipped it on and left with a dark expression on his face.

"Heat?" Yuri asked. "No. I got a very bad feeling about him, though."

"Me too," I said. It was at least partly true. "What kind of a line was that?"

Yuri shrugged. "Perhaps you avoided the bullet."

"Dodged," I murmured. "The phrase is 'dodged the bullet', Yuri."

"It is the same thing," he shot back with total confidence.

From there, we gradually slipped into an argument about idioms, English, and how stubborn Yuri could be about his English skills while we drank the rest of our second beers. We didn't go for a third, and Aaron was kind enough to walk us to the entrance to the upstairs on the street—just in case.

Reece, though, stayed on my mind the rest of the night. Who had he been? Vanity made me want to believe he was hitting on me, maybe. But what if he wasn't? What if he really had wanted to, I don't know, take me to an alley or the bathroom and strangle me? Admittedly that seemed unlikely, but with my history there was just no telling. There were times I thought I was legitimately cursed.

That feeling, though. That strange warmth, and something else. In his eyes, or in his voice—or both. I replayed the encounter over and over until I fell asleep.

And when I dreamed, I dreamed of fire.

Chapter 4
Reece

I had been rash to approach Matthew like that. Something about the smell of him, especially once I was close, had short-circuited the part of my mind that ought to have been more elegant, more careful. He had at least shown some attraction to me, but it seemed that currency had been spent frivolously. Now that I'd ruined my chance to have a face-to-face conversation with him, my only other option was to keep my distance and observe both him and this potential Templar threat.

It meant remaining in the city indefinitely. My own confirmation that Matthew was one of the sacred omegas capable of bearing dragon young wasn't enough. I needed to take him before the ancients, let them see for themselves that our race wasn't doomed to extinction. If they could be swayed, then perhaps the ancient would emerge from their long slumber and actually lead our people again, as tradition dictated.

So I extended the rental agreement on my automobile, and camped out in it a block away from Matthew's home. Far enough that no one would likely notice me, but within sight if I shifted my eyes subtly behind a pair of sunglasses. If there is one thing a dragon is good at, it is sitting motionless and waiting. Some of the ancients had been doing it for going on a millennium.

I didn't have to sit still very long. Dusk and dawn came and went, chasing one another around the Earth, and some hours after the last traces of gold were gone from the sky Matthew emerged from his building with a suitcase in tow.

Had I so affected him that he planned to leave? My instinct was to rush to him, try again, and assure him that I meant him no harm. However, my brief interaction the night before was enough of a lesson to teach me that this was the worst possible course of action. Instead I started the car as he reached the end of the block, and followed at a distance. Ultimately, his journey led him by bus and then train car to the airport.

Keeping watch over him would be more difficult if he boarded a plane. I returned my rental car early, and didn't bother to argue with the agent over the nonrefundable nature of the extension, then went into the airport with my senses alert, seeking out Matthew's earth-and-cinnamon scent among the masses. With so many more people, it was more difficult but fate was, perhaps, in my favor. He was in line, waiting to check his suitcase, on his phone as he chatted with someone and made critical faces they couldn't see.

Careful not to draw attention, I moved to a row of seats by the windows facing the ever-moving lines of cars spilling passengers onto the sidewalks, and carefully shifted my inner ears until the near-useless membranes and organs of the human ear were replaced by the vastly superior faculties of my draconic form. The noise of the place assaulted me at once, but I turned my head slowly and sought out Matthew's voice amid the commotion. As soon as I noticed his distinctive, smooth timbre, I pushed all the rest of it out of the way until I could hear him as though he were next to me.

"…reminding myself to sign up for that TSA pre-approval thing but I always get here late and I'm always in a hurry. Which is ironic, because then I have to stand in line for half an hour." He grunted with some effort. "All right, I made it to the kiosk, I gotta get my tickets and pay for my suitcase. Yeah, I know, but just in case. No, I didn't pack a… Yuri, I don't own a thong. No, I don't. How do you know what's in my underwear drawer? Ew, no, Yuri I threw that out—that was you? Jesus, I thought it was one of Rex's that I somehow still had. Well, then don't sneak things into my underwear drawer, I don't need you meddling and I'm not a stripper. All right, I'm gonna let you go. I'll call you when I get there. Please get laid while I'm gone, the pressure of being your vicarious sex life is overwhelming and very strange. Yeah, I will, love you too."

Love? I pondered that. Nothing about their demeanor before led me to believe they were mated. Though, humans were unusual in their mating habits. They might have many partners over a lifetime, and sometimes more than one at a time. That was a potential complication that I filed away as I followed the sound of Matthew's footsteps and the beating of his heart as it moved through the circuitous route from the kiosk to the counter and widened my focus to listen to the sounds around him.

"Matthew Stiles?" a woman asked. "ID, please. Thank you. San Antonio flight 3211?"

"San Antonio," he agreed. "And then to Catarina, which is even less appealing if you can believe it."

The woman only gave a soft grunt. There was a metallic clunk, and the tearing of paper, but I withdrew my senses at that point. I knew where he was going, and that was all that I needed to know. If I left quickly, I could likely make it there before he arrived. What was more, Texas was an ideal territory to attempt a second introduction. While there were no ancients so far south, there were elders among the mesas who had the necessary dignity that could get them, and myself, an audience with one of them—or their subordinates, at least.

And the weather would most assuredly be warmer and drier.

I stopped by a tourist stand near the exit from the airport, where a tan-skinned young woman smiled politely at me and then seemed to smolder briefly as she looked me over. "How can I help you, sir?"

With some effort, I managed to make myself somewhat friendlier than I had with Matthew. "If you can," I said as I rested an elbow on the counter between us, "could you show me where Catarina, Texas, is located?"

Her smile stiffened but the corner of mouth tugged into a different sort of smile as her eyebrows knit ever so slightly. "It's possible you're in the wrong airport, sir. This is Oregon."

"I'm aware," I assured her. "My next stop is Catarina. I just need a sense of the… lay of the land, if you will."

Her eyes flicked to my shoulder and then down as if she were peeking over the edge of the counter. "Okay… one moment."

She took her phone out and tapped rapidly on the screen. A second later, she turned and showed me an image of a map.

"May I?" I asked as I held a hand out for the device.

"Sure," she said. "Don't run off with it."

I didn't intend to be in human form long enough to have a long-term, practical use for such a thing. I pinched the screen as I'd seen others do to get a better, higher look at the landscape and committed it to memory. If there was one innovation of the most recent age that I found particularly useful, it was this—a dragon's-eye view of the world at one's fingertips. I could follow the magnetic lines to familiar territory, and then search for landmarks that would lead me to Catarina rather than landing to ask directions.

In the old days, going anywhere new was a matter of reaching one dragon and then another, traveling a network of contacts who all had different requirements of courtesy on top of the code of traditions that all dragons were bound to when traveling the territory of another.

This was far more efficient.

I took a cab away from the airport and up to the river, where the driver gave me a queer look as I paid him and got out at the edge of the highway, though he insisted that we drive further up where it wouldn't be such a long walk to anything.

When he was gone, I hopped the low cement wall that separated the highway from the Columbia River and descended the slope to the banks.

When in such a populated area, there are really only two safe places to return to one's scales. High mountains—which the region did have in some abundance but they would take hours to get to in an automobile—and deep waters. Places where humans could not see us change. Once out of my human skin, staying unseen would be a simple matter of illusion, but while wearing this form my magic was out of reach. One did not become human without giving up a great deal of the dragon.

The water was bitterly cold, but I gritted my teeth and waded into it, calling up just enough of my fire to keep myself warm as the water swallowed me up to the shoulders and tugged at this diminutive shape that was ever at the mercy of elements. With a last deep breath, I slipped forward and slid beneath the water. My feet left the rocky bottom, and in seconds I was swept west, toward the sea.

Returning to my true form was like finally relieving a cramp that had plagued me for weeks. I opted to at least keep my size to about half its true extent, and sighed with ecstasy into the freezing river as the human Reece melted away and released my great arms tipped with deadly claws, my magnificent wings that split the current of the water like wind, and the long, graceful tail that streamed behind me as I turned to face upriver. I could finally open my jaw properly, and gulped down water to fill a belly that had become parched from pretending to be so small.

The moment I felt the last of me slip into place, I wrapped my scales in magic that tingled over me and willed it to shroud me from sight. A familiar *click* of the simple enchantment taking hold, and with the thrill of freedom shivering through me, I flicked my tail and raised my head, angling my wings until the current of the Columbia pushed me up and out of the water. Four flaps, and I was free of it and in the air. Another dozen, and I caught the upper, ever mobile air and the tug of a nearby magnetic line pointed south, wrapped in magic and the joy of the flight.

The journey to Catarina was long, but the hours passed quickly. Once the air grew warmer, and I was able to find a high current of air moving south along the middle of the continent, I barely had a need to speed myself along, instead languidly riding the wind at high speed, my fore- and hindlegs pressed tight along my body. Only once did I pause, long enough to snatch up a deer from a field and sate a gnawing hunger left over from spending too long in human skin.

The lush green of the northwest turned to scrub desert, and to forests, and mountains, and then vast desert in shades of red and black and, where the mountains reached highest, remnants of winter's white. The landscape was washed pale when I at last reached Texas, bleaching the mix of red and green that I remembered from more than fifty years before to a pale, moonlit landscape of shadows. Catarina was a mote of light amid the darkness, and easy to find. I tucked my wings and plummeted into a dark, empty patch of land just east of the lights and caught the air just before the ground rose up to strike me. A crack of gentle thunder echoed away, and returned to me the sounds of barking dogs and baying cattle.

It was with no small amount of disappointment and irritation that I released the concealment enchantment and willed my dragon form away, shimmering with feylight as the comfort of wings and tail, claws and teeth, and strength that made a human form seem dangerously vulnerable all shimmered out of existence and left me chilled. The desert night was cold, but at least it was dry.

I oriented myself west, and started walking. Matthew would have a drive ahead of him, or would arrive in a smaller plane to one of the handful of airfields I had seen as I surveyed the area from the sky. Either way, the town of Catarina was so small that I doubted there were many options for lodging.

When I reached the heart of the town, which seemed to be barely a hundred paces from its edge, I sought out the only building in sight that had lights on. A gas station. Inside the attendant offered me a bored look as I pushed through the doors.

That look changed to mild annoyance when I approached him. "Can I help you?"

"I'm looking for lodging," I told him. "What are my options?"

He squinted at me as if perhaps English wasn't his language of choice, though he could not have been paler or of more British stock. "Lodging," he repeated.

"A place where I may exchange currency for temporary shelter," I clarified.

"Like a hotel," he suggested.

I could feel scales rippling along the back of my other body. "Yes," I said with contained acid, "like a hotel."

He shrugged and waved vaguely north. "There's the inn uptown. North on Catarina. On the left. Can't really miss it. Not much else there. You'll go around a curve after the road runs straight on. It'll be 'bout halfway."

"Is there any other place?" I asked.

The attendant shook his head. "Nope. Not a lot of call for it. Not exactly a tourist destination."

Well, that at least simplified things. I turned to leave and heard the human whisper under his breath, "Coulda asked Google, asshole."

So freshly out of my scales, I had to fight an instinct to bring the human to heel, and instead focused on my purpose here. It was not to eat anyone, but to watch over a precious resource to my people.

It was not a long walk to reach the Tropic Inn and Suites, a place that seemed to have forgotten where in the world it was. The night clerk took his headphones only halfway off as I approached, and asked no questions when I requested a room. There was no shortage of options. "Ground floor," I told him as my one requirement.

He accepted cash, which was all that I had, and passed me a key without comment before returning to his computer screen and slipping his headphones back on. The quiet moans of a human woman were just audible, even to my inefficient human ears.

The room had a smell like stale chemical flowers, and the bed was firm enough that in my dragon form it would have been quite comfortable—not so different from the floor of a cave. To my human body, it was an irritant—but I did not intend to sleep. Instead, I parted the curtains facing the parking lot, cracked the window an inch so that I could take in scents from the air outside, and sat down in the thin-bottomed chair to watch, and wait for my sacred omega to arrive.

Chapter 5
Matthew

When I stepped off the ten-passenger plane into the freezing air of a Texas night, I had to uncurl my stomach from around itself to walk steadily again. *Please, God, let there be a rental car place in this tiny town so that I can drive back to San Antonio.* I collected my bag from the pilot-slash-baggage handler with a gracious smile that I hoped said, "Thank you so much for not crashing all five times that I was certain we were going to die."

He didn't smile back. Ah, well. I doubted we were going to become close friends. Speaking of, I leaned on my suitcase and shot Yuri a text, letting him know I made it safely to the back-end of nowhere.

A few minutes later, a minivan took me and my two companion passengers away from the tiny ranch airport and rattled its way along the twenty minutes to town.

My back hurt, my legs and feet hurt, my head pounded behind my eyes, and the bumpy ride into town only made it worse. I began to wonder if I was truly cut out for the field paleontology life. One didn't often dig up dinosaurs in the comfort of the big city.

By the time we pulled up to the only hotel in town—which was decorated with palm trees like some mockery of a tropical vacation spot—I craved sleep, and silently cursed Professor Taylor for offering me ten thousand dollars *just to show up*, but not springing for at least business-class seats or a direct flight. It could have been worse, of course; I could have taken a bus.

I checked in with a desk attendant that I swear was watching porn behind the counter, and slogged the short distance to my room praying silently for a bed that wasn't one of those awful hotel slabs of concrete. Just as I turned the key in the door, my phone buzzed.

"Hey, Yuri," I answered.

"You made it! How is Katrina?"

"It's Catarina," I corrected, "and I have seen exactly a hundred and fifty square feet of it. It has a hotel, at the very least. The flight was awful. Two stops, just enough time to be exhausting but not enough time to get a drink or something."

I left my suitcase by the door and approached the bed dubiously, then gave it a test with one hand. Yep. Concrete.

"I am imagining a hotel full of naked cowboys," Yuri said. "Lounging in the reception area and telling you how little rind you have on you."

I chuckled softly. "You would be mistaken."

"Indulge my fantasy," he insisted. "How many are there?"

"A hundred," I muttered and tested the bed with my ass instead. Nope, still impossible to sleep on. This would be fun. "They're all sweaty, and naked except for boots, chaps, and Stetsons, and I guess I should let you go because like ten of them just flashed their giant cocks at me and I need to go lube up."

"Have fun!" Yuri bade me with a cackle. We said our goodbyes and I hung up and gave the bed a long, baleful glare that I hoped would somehow soften it.

It did not, but it was already almost midnight. Taylor was supposed to send a driver for me in the morning, early, so there was hardly any point in sleeping well anyway. A quick nip out to the wilderness and back and I'd be ten thousand dollars flush and hopefully on my way home in something that wouldn't threaten to drop out of the sky every fifteen minutes.

I flopped onto the bed, squirmed around and readjusted the pillows, got up to take two Tylenol in hopes that my back wouldn't be too sore in the morning, and then lay silently staring at the ceiling while I waited to fall asleep.

Three hours later, I ached and was nowhere near sleeping.

I sat up and elected to make coffee instead, and unpacked my laptop while it brewed. God willing, Professor Taylor had a camp set up with literally anything that was remotely more comfortable than the bed here. I opened up the university website and scanned the listings for potential job openings. After I was done here, I had some room to breathe but needed to get something—anything—lined up.

Before the coffee finished brewing, the handle of the door to my room rattled softly. I froze, and watched the door. Had I locked it? They must have had a late night check-in and somehow given someone the wrong room number. It rattled again, a bit more forcefully this time. I got up and walked to the door. The peephole was dark and useless. "There's someone in here," I called through the door.

The rattling stopped.

No one outside spoke at all, much less offered an apology for presumably waking me up.

I relaxed muscles that I only then realized were tense, and left the door and the rude would-be intruder to go back to my computer and the never-ending search for something to justify my student loans.

Halfway across the room, I jumped almost out of my skin as the door burst in.

Instantly, all thought left my brain and all I had to hold onto was abject panic. I whipped around to see two large men in dark hoodies, gloved, and with the bit of light streaming in from between the curtains caught the glint of metal in their hands.

I never knew how I would react to a situation like this. Turns out, between fight and flight, my body picks fight. Maybe I have Rex to thank for that.

The first thing within reach was the coffee pot. I snatched it by the handle and hurled it at the two men. Fresh-brewed coffee splashed over both of them and the pot struck the taller of the two men in the shoulder before falling and shattering on the floor. They hissed curses as the hot coffee burned, but it only slowed them for a second.

By then, I'd managed to throw the coffee maker itself at them, and was pulling out a drawer from the small dresser to throw that as well. Something inside told me to just keep piling stuff up at and between them until they went away or something did damage.

The man in front rushed me, though, and kicked the drawer closed. The wood scraped out of my fingers, and I fell back as he swung that knife at my neck. I tripped, knocked over the table, and scrambled to grab my laptop as he knelt and plunged the knife down at me.

It glanced off the chassis of the laptop and slipped to one side, cutting my hand in the bargain, and with a howl of defiance that I didn't intentionally summon, I kicked him hard between the legs.

"Fuck," he groaned, and then gave only a wheezing grunt of shock as I kicked him again, and again, until he stumbled back and sagged against the wall, clutching at his nuts with both hands. The knife. He'd dropped the knife. Where was it?

I spotted it between us and lunged to my feet to dive for it. Not fast enough. The second man was already close. He kicked the knife and with one hand grabbed a handful of hair to haul me to my feet. I grabbed his hand by instinct to try and dislodge him, but he reared back his knife hand and a cold kind of fear I had never even dreamed existed spread through me. Time seemed to slow, but didn't offer me any special insight. No last minute brilliance. I had fought, and lost, and was going to die. Flight probably was the better option for someone who'd never actually had the guts to get into a real fight before.

Instead of plunging the metal into my guts, however, the man's arm stopped as a shape loomed up behind him. There was a sound of something wet breaking, and he screamed as the hand holding my hair let go. I stumbled back as his body spun around and then went hurtling across the room and into the far wall by the window. He slumped, and the dark figure moved like death itself to intercept him while I scrambled away to safety between the nightstand and the wall. My hand brushed the fallen knife and I clutched it close, shaking uncontrollably as the shadow planted its fist into the recovering attacker whose balls I had tried to crush.

That man fell, unconscious or dead, while the other pushed off the wall unsteadily and threw himself into a tackle.

The shadow man caught him under the chin and lifted him sharply up. The attacker's lower body kept moving as he turned horizontal in the air, went heels over head, and clattered in a heap to the floor. With a grunt of effort, the shadow man stomped, and the attacker went quiet.

For several seconds, the sound of my rapid breathing and the pounding of my heart made the room too loud. The man took a step toward me. I thrust the knife out at him. "Don't!"

He paused, and held his hands up. "I'm not going to hurt you."

The voice was familiar, deep and resonating, but my thoughts were so panicked and tangled I couldn't think of where I'd heard it before. "Leave me alone!"

He approached despite my undoubtedly fearsome visage, crouched like a scared rabbit in a corner, and kept his hands spread as he knelt so that the light from the window caught his face. "Matthew, you're safe now," he said. "It's me. Reece. From the bar. Do you remember me?"

A whole new flavor of panic entered the field, tumbling down a slope of maddening confusion. "I... you... Reece from the bar?" I shook my head, gasping for air and unable to get anywhere near enough into my lungs. "What the hell are you doing here? How did you... why are you... I... I can't..."

I couldn't breathe, even with my lungs pumping so hard that I could stop them. The knife was still pointed at him, but it shook like there should have been an earthquake beneath us.

And a lot of good it did. Reece reached slowly toward me, and closed his hand over mine. "I can help you. Just breathe."

I started to pull my hand away, but his grip was stronger than his gentleness implied. "Don't touch me, I—"

Warmth poured into me from my hand, thick and syrupy. With it came a kind of what I can only call a sense of safety. It didn't immediately clear my mind, but my body drank it in like opium, craving more once it got the first taste, and my lungs stopped pumping so desperately. I was given back control, and could take long, shuddering breaths as my heart slowed and that warm sense of security drove off the adrenaline that had taken charge.

I let him take the knife from my hand, and he tucked it away into his coat. He pulled at my wrist until I cooperated with him and stood.

"We have to get away from here," he said. "Did you pay with a cash?"

"What?" I couldn't understand why it mattered.

"Cash," he repeated. "Did you give the man downstairs cash?"

I nodded dumbly.

"There will have been cameras," Reece muttered. He tugged me to him, and I remembered this feeling—this strange heat that he radiated that seemed to reach into me and warm something I didn't know was there before. I wanted to throw my arms around him, hold onto him and beg him to keep me safe.

Reece did not embrace me, though. He turned and urged me ahead of him. "There is a door down the hallway, unlocked. At the end, on the right. Go in there, stay quiet, and wait for me."

I turned to face him. "Why are you here?"

"I followed you," he said simply. "Or, rather, I knew where you would be, and waited for you."

"That's not a comforting answer, Reece," I hissed. "*Why* are you here?"

He glanced down at the two bodies. "I should expect that to be obvious," he said. "You were just attacked. I intervened. I came to protect you."

"From who?" I demanded. "Who are these men?"

Reece sighed. "They will not be alone, so we need to move quickly. But they are Templars, Matthew. And they will not stop at this to kill you or me."

And with those words my world turned inside out, and never returned to normal.

Chapter 6
Reece

Once Matthew was sequestered in my room, I went about cleaning up the mess. No one could doubt that there was violence done in his room, but at this hour neither did anyone notice when I hauled the two bodies, one by one, out of the hotel and into the darkness, my ears half-shifted to keep part of my attention on Matthew. The walls of the building made his movement in the room faint, but he paced endlessly, his footsteps beating like a frightened heart on the floor.

I undressed each body and found, just as Tarin's photos indicated, the sign of the Templars on their chests. How had they known he was coming here? In the past, they had vast networks of spies and informants. Perhaps they had recovered their numbers sufficiently, and in secret, these long centuries since their fall that they had such resources to hand.

Once the bodies were undressed, and I could hear no other humans in the region, I shifted into the smallest dragon form I could manage, the size of a horse perhaps, and incinerated the two Templars until even their bones were ash, then clawed at the ground to mix them with the hard soil before packing myself back into my human form.

I found Matthew still pacing when I returned.

"Where did you go?" he demanded. "I left my phone in the room, I have to get it—"

"It is possible they found you by means of that device," I told him. "It would be better if it was left here."

He gaped at me. "I can't just leave it. We have to call the police and tell them—"

"Law enforcement is ill advised," I said quickly. "I have disposed of the bodies."

He froze, staring at me with wide eyes, his jaw working slowly. "You... did *what*?"

"They will not be found, I assure you," I said as I went to the window and checked what my ears had already suggested—that there were no more, as of the moment, Templars gathered outside waiting to see how the assassination fared. They had sent only two, it seemed.

"Someone always finds the body, Reece—and also, I'm not concerned about someone finding them, they tried to kill me. I have to—"

I turned and took him by the arms, careful not to harm him in doing so, and let just a touch of my fire brush him. As with all sacred omegas, his body responded. I was careful—only enough to calm him, not so much as to bond with him. Though even this small contact stirred that desire in my chest, and in my groin.

A sacred omega. In my very grasp. It was dangerous, an invitation for disaster and consequences that could last centuries if I mishandled this.

I focused my mind, calmed the instinct to claim him and sow my seed in him. That was not my right; even if he was the only one in the world, and even if the ancients didn't know—everyone would know of a hatchling dragon eventually, and would wonder why I had kept such a monumental secret to myself and defied law and tradition by taking him for myself.

"Reece…"

I licked my lips and let him go. "I apologize," I muttered as I turned away to consider carefully how best to approach a conversation he was in no way prepared for. When I turned back, he had wrapped his arms around himself and looked so very afraid that I considered skipping explanations to sweep him up in my dragon form and carry him to one of my caves.

They were ill suited to human habitation at the moment, however. And the trouble that would summon was incalculable.

"Why did you come to Catarina?" I asked.

He blinked, confused, and shook his head slowly. "You knew I was coming here but didn't know why?"

"I overheard you at the airport," I explained.

That didn't clear anything up, apparently. Matthew only shook his head again but finally waved a hand at the window. "There's a dig here. I'm a paleontologist. Or I'm trying to be, anyway. One of my old professors flew me down, he's found something and wants me to confirm it for him. Probably because no one else will. He's a little… anyway, does this matter?"

"Digging for bones," I murmured. "Where is it?"

"East of here," Matthew said.

"Remote?" I asked.

He shrugged. "Ah… I guess so."

It wasn't the worst possible location. Templars congregated in cities and towns, where once they had established keeps and outposts and secret temples in the great cities of the old world. They were not bandits to rove the countryside unless there was a dragon to hunt. "Who else knows of this? Of where you're going?"

Matthew shrugged. "My friend, Yuri. He doesn't know exactly where—oh, God, is he in danger as well?"

"No," I said. "No, they are looking specifically for you. Everyone else, they will endeavor to hide themselves from. That is who they are. Shadows, hiding in the darkness for the unwary. They cannot risk drawing too much attention to themselves. I suspect this is why they came for you here, rather than in the city. They were waiting for you to be more isolated, out of reach."

Matthew sank to the edge of the bed. "They knew I was here," he breathed. "They were following me… they knew when I left. How long has this been going on? What am I supposed to do? We have to call the police, or the FBI, or someone who can—"

This again. Mortals and law enforcement. I pulled a chair away from the small table so that I could sit facing him, and held my hands out until he cautiously placed his in them. I closed my fingers gently around his hands and gave him the touch of my fire again as I spoke. "Matthew, you must listen to me now," I said softly, as his eyes rose to meet mine. "The people that are after you are unknown to your law officers. If you go to them, they will not believe you. The Templars are long dead, so we thought. Now, they are a curiosity of history, and in their age they were believed to be virtuous. Heroes of the people, a sacred order of the church. You will get no help from constables. You must trust me in this, though I know you have little reason. I swear to you, I will protect you from these men. You are precious beyond your understanding, and if it required that I die in the bargain, my life would be well spent."

Matthew's eyebrows knit slowly as I spoke, and when I finished, he opened his mouth as if to speak but only stared at me for a long moments before he closed it and tried again. "Uh... I don't... what is that? That feeling. Every time you touch me, it's like something changes inside. What is it? What... what are you?"

"Your guardian," I said. "What you feel is a deep knowledge of that. That I will keep you safe."

He gave a small nod, and his tense hands and arms relaxed. "Then what do we do next?"

"I believe," I said as I let his hands go and placed them in his lap, "that we may fare best by going to this place you originally planned. The land east of here is open, it will be difficult for anyone to approach unnoticed. I may be able to contact others, but do not wish to attempt it until you are secure. It is a delicate situation. Do you know the way?"

Matthew shrugged. "I'm supposed to be picked up tomorrow. Or, I suppose, today. I have a vague idea but I couldn't drive there."

"What time?" I asked.

"Six thirty. Just a few hours." He glanced at the clock. "Fuck. Like an hour and a half, actually."

"I will accompany you," I told him. "You will be safe under my watch. You should rest."

He gave the bed a skeptical look and grimaced. "Um... I don't think I can. I should get cleaned up. I need my suitcase from my room. It's got clothes and... maybe it doesn't matter, but it's just all I've got with me, so..."

I stood. His room was nearby, there would be little danger leaving him alone for under a minute, though I had to remind myself of that when my instinct was to insist that we not leave the room at all until it was time to leave. "Wash yourself here," I said. "I will retrieve your suitcase."

He eyed me, a mix of curiosity and weak amusement. "You have a really odd way of saying things. Where are you from?"

"Arizona," I answered. That's what the territory was called commonly these days.

Matthew barked a laugh, and covered his mouth quickly to stymie the rest of it. He waved a hand. "Sorry, sorry. I shouldn't... did you make a joke?"

I shook my head. "I did not."

He took a long breath, and bobbed his head as he stood. "Okay then. Reece from Arizona. I guess… it's nice to meet you properly."

"I wish it were under more auspicious circumstances, Matthew," I said.

Matthew bit his lip, his lips attempting to curl into another grin. At least he was recovered in part from his ordeal. I returned it to signal that I was not offended by his amusement, and the grin escaped his control. He rounded the corner of the bed and headed to the lavatory, giving me a final glance before he disappeared through the doorway and closed the door behind him.

Briefly, I imagined him undressing. The thoughts came unbidden to me. I let them linger only a moment before brushing them away. There were more important matters to tend to than my breeding instincts.

Chapter 7
Matthew

It was a quiet wait after I showered, and felt longer than an hour. I wanted so badly to call Yuri, let him know what was going on, but if Reece was right about these… *Templars*… somehow tracking me by my phone then for all I knew it was tapped, and maybe Yuri's was as well, and for all I knew they were opening my mail. Reasoning through all that didn't lessen the desire, but it at least kept me from dialing his number on the hotel phone.

That, and I hadn't memorized a number since I was eight years old.

So I wrung my hands, paced, and watched Reece stand almost inhumanly motionless at the window, watching the parking lot.

It should have freaked me out more. This man had approached me in a bar, asking to speak to me privately when I didn't know who the hell he was. Then he apparently followed me over two thousand miles to show up at just the right moment to save me from a pair of thugs bent on killing me. What world was I in? Not the one I belonged in. Not remotely close to it.

I was no one. A guy with an expensive master's degree and a lot of debt—why would anyone want to kill me? My parents were no one, they'd come from people who were, in turn, nobodies. Probably that went all the way back to the dawn of time. I was boring, my family was boring, my ancestors had been boring since they came across the Atlantic and very likely a long time before. What was the point of coming after me?

"Can you at least tell me why me?" I asked Reece when I couldn't stand it anymore.

"It may be better that you not know yet," he answered, and left it at that.

The man had a strange effect on me, something warm and comforting and magnetic—but he was still frightening. Predatory in some way I couldn't put my finger on aside from his size and the preternatural stillness he was capable of. The two instincts warred inside me. Go to him, or run from him? Every time he looked at me, it gave me a shiver of fear and, if I was being honest… desire.

That, I told myself, was entirely natural. I had been through something traumatic. He had interrupted my murder. Some part of my psyche identified him as a safe place, and because I had a history of insecurity attached to romantic entanglements, the two things shared space in my brain and made it hard to tell the difference. Easy-peasy pop psychology.

Knowing it, or at least theorizing it, didn't change anything. Stupid psyche.

Finally, a car pulled up outside. Reece bristled into movement, letting out a low growl as he took a step back from the window. I rushed to him and without looking he put out a hand to block me. "Wait."

I could see the beat-up old Jeep, though, and the tired-looking, dirt-caked intern—only an intern would have been sent on an errand like this—pulling out her phone. She was slender, with a narrow face and a mound of dreadlocks on her head, barely contained under a bandana. "That's my ride," I told

Reece. "And she's trying to call me but I don't have my phone. Look at her, she's fresh off the dig site. God, I'm guessing that means the showers are rare and spare."

Reece glanced back at me, watched the girl press the phone to her ear and patiently wait for an answer that wasn't going to come. He grunted assent finally, and closed the curtain as I went for my suitcase.

With Reece in tow, I rushed out the back entrance at his insistence and circled around to meet the woman at her Jeep, waving as I approached. "Hi! I'm here, I'm here. Sorry. I saw you pull up. Uh… lost my phone at the airport."

The woman lowered the phone and stuffed it into the front of her overalls before she hopped out of the vehicle and scurried around to help with the suitcase.

"That's okay, I…" but she snatched it before I could stop her.

"You must be Matthew Stiles," she chirped as she hefted the suitcase into the back. When it was secured, she scampered back to me and stuck a hand out. I took it and she shook with both of hers. Vigorously. "I'm so excited to meet you. Doc talks about you all the time, he has a lot of respect for you. And I can't wait for you to see what we found. Oh, I'm Mercy. Mercy Brave. I'm Doc's assistant."

"His assistant," I said, bewildered and a little overwhelmed. I chalked it up to lack of sleep and almost being murdered. "I figured he'd send an intern."

"Oh, no," she said quickly, shaking her head and, still, my hand. "No, we don't have… it's a very competitive field, you know."

No interns. Naturally. Because none of them would be taken seriously and the credit under Professor Taylor wouldn't be worth much on a resume. It made me wonder where on Earth he'd found Mercy.

Mercy's eyes finally drifted to Reece.

"Oh, this is Reece," I said, catching her eye. "He's, ah…"

"Your partner?" There was a hint of hopefulness in her voice.

"No," I said at the same time Reece affirmed, "Yes."

"Business… partner," I clarified. "He's a consultant that I work with a lot. On…"

"Natural history," Reece supplied smoothly. "I heard about the project and was considerably enticed. I'm quite familiar with this region."

"A twofer," Mercy said, grinning as she shook Reece's hand as well, though not for as long and not as wildly as she had mine. "Fantastic. I'm sure Doc would love to talk to you."

I spared Reece a look that I hoped said *"We need to get our stories straight when we have a chance."*

When he only smiled slightly at me, I decided I was not a master of spy-like body language or telepathy. We piled into the Jeep with Mercy, and started the drive east.

"Doc says you were a student of his," Mercy said as we pulled out of Catarina and onto a barely paved road.

"I was," I said. "About eight years ago, my sophomore year. Were you?"

She laughed. "No, I didn't exactly matriculate traditionally."

Good God, was it that bad? Who exactly was funding a dig and hiring amateurs? "How interesting," I said. "So what exactly do you do? I mean, aside from being Taylor's assistant. What's your, um, area of expertise?"

Mercy shrugged. "What isn't? I'm an herbalist, a doula, an astrologer, an expert in crystal healing. Oh, and an expert draconologist."

"A draconologist?" Reece asked from the back seat. "You study… dragons?"

She grinned at him in the rearview mirror. "Yes, sir! It's not an official course of study in traditional colleges, of course, but I've been fascinated with them since I was little. Do you know virtually every culture in the world has some kind of dragon story in their cultural canon of folklore?"

"I was not aware," Reece muttered.

"Hm?" Mercy glanced back at him.

"I said that's very interesting," he said louder.

I turned to search his face for some sign of mockery, but saw only a flat affect and hard eyes boring into the back of Mercy's head.

"So you've had a… diverse career, it sounds like," I pushed, changing the subject. "How exactly did you end up with Taylor?"

"We met at a convention," Mercy said. We merged onto a highway, and the ride became smoother. "It's a pretty short drive, only about forty-five minutes."

"Great," I said. "What convention, exactly?"

"Creature Weekend." She flicked a convention badge hanging from the mirror along with a few crystals, a small leather pouch, and various religious charm icons on a long silver chain. "It's a cryptozoology conference. Last year there was a big presentation on dragons. We were in the front row and Doc had some remarkably insightful questions for the panel—which, really, he should have been on, if you ask me—and afterward we had a few drinks and he invited me to help him on a dig."

I let that settle in for a moment. "Mercy," I asked, "does Professor Taylor believe he's digging up a dragon?"

She gave a wry, secretive smile. "Afraid I can't answer that," she said, and winked at me. "NDAs and all that. The person funding this project has got beaucoup bucks and is pouring a lot into this. Totally private because of course all the academics think we're bonkers." She waved a finger around her temple and *cackled*.

My career is over before it began, I thought. "How lucky."

"He as yet has no proof that he is unearthing a dragon, though," Reece said.

"I didn't confirm what we're digging up," Mercy countered. "But let's just say we have some compelling discoveries. You'll hear all about it when we arrive. Believe me, Doc doesn't talk about anything else!"

I glanced back again to see Reece's flat expression replaced by something far darker, and had to wonder—what the hell did he care about Taylor's dig for?

About half an hour after, I knew far more about Mercy than anyone needs to know about a person, including that her cycle was perfectly synced to the full moon, allegedly thanks to a combination of malachite and moonstone, and that she practiced a mixture of Buddhism, Wicca, and Zoroastrianism. She subscribed to the *sidereal* astrology rather than *tropical*, and had some very compelling reasons why, which she shared with us at length right up to the point that we arrived at a wide circle of metal-sided campers that enclosed a large, sand-colored canvas tent.

I could not have gotten out of the Jeep faster, and was never more happy for a car to have no doors on it.

"What a fun drive!" Mercy exclaimed as she hauled my suitcase out of the back and extended the handle for me. "I think you're going to fit in really well here, both of you. So happy to have you! Let me show you to your camper. Um… we didn't expect an extra guest, so there's just the one but I'm sure Taylor can have another one brought out?"

I waved a hand to dismiss it as I didn't intend to stay for more than a few days. "That would be—"

"Unnecessary," Reece cut in. "We'll be occupying the same camper."

"He just means—"

"It's important that we remain in close proximity to one another," he explained, again cutting me off.

I was left with a tense jaw that I had to consciously relax as I smiled politely at Mercy's widening conspiratorial grin. "To compare notes and… things like that."

"Just so you know," she said, sweeping an arm to include the entire site, "this is a one hundred percent inclusive and accepting place. Everyone here can be who they are, and all are welcome. All genders, and sexualities, and religious—"

"I understand," I said quickly. "That's so very comforting, Mercy. If I could just drop my stuff off and maybe meet with Professor Taylor?"

"Of course! Right this way, fellow adventurer." She turned to march into the ring of campers.

"We don't have to be here long," I told Reece. "Once I see Taylor's findings and present my arguments, we can go wherever we need to. I assume back to the city isn't an option?"

Reece was surveying the place, and the land around us. "This is an ideal location," he said. "I believe remaining here will be a good idea."

He said it with such finality, as if that was the decided course of action, that I held my tongue rather than arguing it for now. I tugged at the suitcase and more dragged it than rolled it over the rough ground, around patches of dry grass, to the cabin that Mercy stopped at and opened the door to. It was small inside, but the bed was of a decent size and took up about a fifth of the cabin at one end. There was a small kitchenette, a bathroom, and a slender closet with two drawers inside. Once I'd looked it over and set the suitcase on the narrow fold-out table, I emerged and gave Mercy's look of expectation a stiff thumbs-up. "Looks just fine. Thanks."

"Well, if you're ready," Mercy said, "Taylor should be in his tent. Come see what we're up to! Goddess, this is so exciting, isn't it?"

I nodded, and we trailed behind her as she made her way around the largest tent—the one covering the dig itself, I suspected, and it was certainly large enough to house a dragon, I imagined. Or more likely some very large cretaceous-era predator like the Tyrannosaurus rex, which was common to North America and made much more sense than a mythological animal that never existed.

Taylor's tent was attached to the main dig tent, set up in an old-world, intrepid adventurer style complete with rugs laid on the floor, a large hardwood table with a map of the region as well as various military-grade-looking laptops, and a tall bookshelf housing his collection of reference books, both well-esteemed and very questionable.

Taylor himself was seated at a smaller desk, scribbling furiously in a notebook that he closed quickly when Mercy cleared her throat. Taylor had grown older, now white-haired and bushy-eyebrowed in just these short years. Not that he'd been young before, but it seemed that the stress of losing his career—his academic career, at least—and working as a field researcher again had taken its toll. Still, he had no trouble springing to his feet. "Matthew, my boy! You made it. I can't—oh, and who is this now?"

"My consultant," I said, plastering on the most professional expression I could under the circumstances. "Reece… Smith. A natural historian."

"A pleasure to be acquainted," Reece said, and offered Taylor a hand.

They shook, and Taylor embraced me briefly with a pat on the back. After, he held me at arm's length by the shoulders. "I'm so happy to have you here. Both of you. I'd love to show you what we're working on, but before that I do need you to sign some papers. Let's not delay."

Taylor led us to the table and produced a folder for me, and had Mercy print another packet. It was fairly standard. The NDA covered a period of two years, conditional on the basis of any published papers. The patron of the project was only named in a bland-sounding corporation that I assumed was some sort of shell of a holding company of another shell to create as much distance as possible from the reputation of whatever eccentric billionaire was throwing their money away. Once Reece and I had both signed the NDAs, waivers, and agreements, and Taylor had a chance to assure Reece that he could probably arrange to pay him his consulting fee—with no mention of checking his credentials, but then Mercy was right there with us after all—he finally opened one of the fancy laptops.

"What you are about to see," he said, "is going to change our very conception of the world. Everything you think you know will change. Everything I thought that *I* knew has changed drastically since this discovery was made. Are you ready to see it?"

Taylor had always had a dramatic streak. I clasped my hands on the table. "Please. I'm beyond excited."

"As am I," Reece said.

Mercy and Taylor shared a grin, and he opened a file on the laptop, then pushed it toward me.

The image was a result of a sonar instrument, grainy but showing relative densities, so that the bones of the creature showed up as a blue-white image surrounded by darker blues and blacks where the soil and surrounding geology was less dense. Scattered throughout were chunks of white that were likely errant bits of rock, but they did not obscure the skeleton itself, and I found myself staring blankly at the screen trying to make sense of what I was looking at. Or rather, to rationalize it.

Because at first glance, just tracing the shape of it and with no other proof, I had to admit even as a skeptic: it looked a hell of a lot like a dragon.

Chapter 8
Reece

It was a dragon.

The humans had discovered the burial site of a dragon. How old it was, and from what clan, I couldn't say just by looking, but the structure of the wings, the proportions of the limbs to the body, and the shape of the skull suggested that it was, in fact, from my own region of origin. There was a chance that these remains were, as a human would put it, a distant family member.

A deep, gnawing sense of unease settled into my stomach. This was very bad. By tradition, the defilement of a dragon's grave was a high crime, regardless of knowledge or ignorance. More than a few such events had resulted in severe reprisals. If the ancients knew of this, the whole of Texas might be razed the ground.

"Can you believe it?" Mercy whispered. "An honest-to-Goddess dragon, right here in Texas. It's the discovery of a lifetime. Of the millennium. Heck, it's the greatest discovery of human history."

"I don't think we should get ahead of ourselves," Matthew said, his eyes still locked on the screen. He traced a finger along various lines of the skeleton. "These fossils could have been dug up elsewhere, rearranged, buried here as a hoax. They're not nearly deep enough in the ground, to start with, what is this—twelve feet?"

Taylor blew out a long, tense breath, and bit his lip as he picked up a folder and passed it to Matthew.

Matthew took it cautiously and opened it, scanning pages and flipping through them before he looked up, incredulous. "What do you mean, not fossilized?"

"I mean," Taylor said, his chest swelling as he straightened and took on a smug look of satisfaction, "that they are not fossils. We've taken samples, run hundreds of tests. These are *bones*, Matthew. We haven't carbon dated yet, and the density makes the post-mortem difficult to assess, but best that we can tell from the geological standpoint, they could be as little as two thousand years old. Or as old as… perhaps ten thousand? Well within the scope of human existence. Do you see what this means? It means that dragons may well have lived among us."

"And for all we know," Mercy added, "they *still* do."

Dragons do not panic. Fear isn't a common emotion to our experience. Even in human form, subject to human ordeals, there is always the knowledge that one can simply shed that form and return to scales and wings and the freedom that an apex predator enjoys from vulnerability.

To see this, though…

Dragons were creatures of myth to most humans because we had hidden ourselves for nearly twelve thousand years. Our images, the memory of a time when the Ancients ruled and demanded sacrifice, had persisted in that time. Our burial grounds were beneath mountains, and in the implacable depths of the oceans. Places no human, we believed, would reach.

Why was there a dragon buried here? And so recently? And how was this land not somehow protected from the possibility of discovery? Moreover, why dig in this place? To find one skeleton, twelve feet under the ground, did not seem like random chance. There had been no earthquake to reveal my kin, nor some great flood to wash away the soil.

"How," I asked, "was the... specimen discovered?"

"As far as I know," Taylor said, "a local was in the area, digging for artifacts that are fairly common to the region, from the Coahuiltecan people who inhabited these lands before colonialization, and came upon a tooth. Word reached our funder, and he sought me out as one of only a few experts in draconological paleontology."

"I was not aware there was such a field," I said.

"Strictly speaking," Taylor mused, "there isn't. Not officially recognized, in any case. After this, I expect I'll be the foremost expert. And also... the only one. But that will change! Where there is one set of remains, there are most assuredly others."

"Assuming this isn't a hoax," Matthew said. He shook his head at the papers and the screen and handed the folder back to Taylor. "I have to admit, it is compelling, Professor. But there are still other possible explanations. Almost all of these bones could belong to other animals. Whales, elephants, big cats. And some of them may still turn out to be fossils, like those claws, and the vertebrae. Until the whole specimen is unearthed and tests are run, I wouldn't be too quick to draw conclusions."

Taylor clapped Matthew on the shoulder. "That's why you're here, my boy. I need a skeptic in this camp who can do everything possible to disprove my findings. Doubt, question, play the devil's advocate at every turn. I am confident in my discovery, and welcome the discourse."

"Matthew has had quite a long day," I said to Taylor and Mercy as Taylor opened his mouth to begin another phase of the introduction and reached for another folder. "Perhaps he should retire for a time, to rest and make himself freshly sharpened for the task ahead."

Taylor, Mercy, and Matthew all turned to give me a queer look of interest and concern. Matthew cleared his throat and addressed the other two humans. "He... is a history buff. They all talk like that in my experience. Um... he's not wrong. I should go lie down, I didn't get much sleep last night. I'll start brainstorming possible tests we can run, Professor. Mercy, it was a pleasure to meet you. I'm... certain we will see one another again soon."

"I should hope so," Mercy beamed. "It's a small camp, we can't really avoid one another!"

"No," Matthew said as he stood. "No, I don't imagine we can."

"Lunch is at one," Taylor called as we left his tent. "We all gather outside the dig for it. You should come, meet the rest of the crew!"

"Will do," Matthew called back without looking.

We walked in silence back to our camper, Matthew with his eyes downcast, his arms folded as if deep in thought, and I attempting to recall the clans and lineages of the area to determine what specific direction an immolation was likely to arrive from. *Coahuiltecan*, Professor Taylor had said... were they among the tribes of Wolven? So much of the formal history of the area had been destroyed, including many of the Wolven. It was entirely possible that all of them had been erased, even if the tribe that sheltered them had survived. Templars were not known for their mercy toward any nonhumans, and genocide had been a tradition for millennia before they were believed to have finally breathed their collective last.

"A dragon," Matthew muttered as he opened the camper door and ascended the creaking steps into it. He leaned against the narrow counter inside. "I mean, it's insane, right? It has to be some kind of hoax."

"I suppose that seems a likely explanation," I agreed.

Perhaps I had not spoken convincingly. Matthew narrowed his eyes at me. "That was unenthused. Don't tell me you believe this stuff. Dragons? Then again, I never imagined I'd be targeted by Templars either. Assuming, of course, those people were who you say they are. How do you know anyway?"

"That a hoax is a likely explanation," I asked, "or that the men who came for you were Templars?"

"Both, I guess," he replied. He pushed off the counter and went to the bed, where he sat on the edge.

I took a seat that the fold-out table, conscious of the closeness of these quarters and already considering where this body would be most comfortable. The floor seemed like the only option other than the bed, and I did not relish the thought. Perhaps I would patrol overnight in my scales; the nights here were undoubtedly black but for the stars and moon. "As you have asserted," I offered, "the existence of a dragon is of course naturally in question. Some artificial construction would seem to be the simplest explanation. As for the Templars…"

How could I isolate the matter of the Templars from the existence of my kind? Matthew raised an eyebrow, waiting with barely contained impatience.

"They bear a mark," I said. "On the chest, over the heart, as a… monument to their oaths."

"Which are?" he pressed.

They had changed somewhat over the ages, but at least one element was consistent. "To protect mankind from the forces of darkness."

Matthew laughed. "Oh. Well, that seems righteous enough. Except, how exactly am *I* a force of darkness?"

"Perhaps their purview has expanded."

He laughed again, and the corner of my mouth tugged up of its own accord. I quickly took back control, but with the door the small space closed, Matthew's enticing scent had quickly filled the space and now teased at the dragon that was hidden by this human flesh. It was not made easier to ignore when he shook his head and then fell slowly back onto the bed, his arms outstretched so that his stomach was exposed.

Millions of years of instincts that were buried inside the very essence of my being could not help but see it as a gesture. One of submission, openness—the ancient signal of readiness to mate. It was made that much worse when he twisted his body one way and the other, groaning with relief as he squirmed further onto the bed and finally opened his jaw wide in a yawn.

I realized I was gripping the edge of the table, and that in my rapt attention I had shifted my claws ever so slightly into existence. Four V-shaped indentations now marked the pale, textured plastic. I withdrew them at once, and folded my hands in my lap.

"You weren't wrong," Matthew said languidly. "I am fucking exhausted. I need just like… like two hours to nap or something. This bed is so much more comfortable than that slab of rock they had at the inn."

"Of course," I said, standing from the seat and smoothing my suit.

Matthew craned his neck to peer at me. "You must be tired, too."

"I require very little sleep." I went to the door to leave the tight space and that maddening scent of his, and stand guard outside.

Matthew pushed up on his elbows and gave me a long, thoughtful look. I returned it, sensing that he meant to speak, and waited.

"I… don't know about Templars," he said at last. "But I didn't say thank you, before. For rescuing me like that. Not that it's okay to go around stalking people, okay? But… I'm glad you were there. And I guess I'm glad you're here, too. It makes me feel safer. So. Thanks."

"You are welcome," I replied.

He licked his lips. "You can, um… I mean, if you did want to get just a little rest. This bed is big enough for both of us, I think. There's an extra blanket in the closet, not that you really need it in this oven. And two pillows. More comfortable than the floor, obviously. Just if you wanted, I don't want you to think that you have to like… camp outside or something."

A new smell drifted through the cabin. Sweat. From the heat, but also from some new element of chemistry that Matthew could not have been aware of. Readiness. Need. One hand drifted to his stomach and rested there, and his breathing came quicker.

I forced myself to tug the handle of the door. "I should… examine the perimeter of this encampment. Become familiar with possible routes of ingress. Rest, Matthew. It would be better if you were alert."

He only nodded, and lay back down as I left the camper.

I looked down at my human body, and mentally scolded it for being so obvious in its arousal.

Humans. Utterly lacking in subtlety.

Chapter 9
Matthew

I desperately wanted to talk to Yuri, if for no other reason than to have the comfort of his laughter when I told him how badly I had bombed that stupid attempt at seduction. I could already hear him, *"Matthew,"* he would say, *"men are unsubtle creatures. You should have gotten to your knees and invited him to sex by putting your mouth on his cock."* Or something similar, anyway. Yuri was the type of guy who, when he wanted someone, he just went and got them. And it worked for him. Every time.

Of course, Yuri was also petite, and chock full of confidence, and had startling blue eyes that made every guy he looked at come in their pants, so. He didn't exactly have to struggle to make himself seen, and everyone just assumed his intentions were to fuck them. Because they generally *were*.

Reece hadn't been wrong to say I needed rest. I did. Badly. But my mind was spinning with the thousand possibilities now assailing me from all sides. There were people called Templars who were after me, possibly in some quest to fight "the forces of darkness" whatever *that* meant. As skeptical as I was, there was the possibility—however remote—that Professor Taylor had, somehow, managed to find an actual dragon skeleton. I was 99 percent certain that this was not the case, of course. After all, I'd seen mermaid skeletons, unicorns, three-headed dogs, and all manner of other hoaxes that were convincingly played but ultimately debunked. But that one percent did eat at me. What *if* it was real? It really would turn the world upside down.

And on top of all that, there was *Reece*.

I turned onto my side, closed my eyes and tried to will my thoughts to slow, and leave me alone, and let me sleep. I hummed to myself, and tried to get a lullaby stuck in my head, and when that failed I tried to get a Katie Perry song in there instead. When that didn't work, I went for "Karma Chameleon," and it did work for a little bit but the drone of it in my brain wasn't loud enough to keep everything else out.

I flipped to my other side, and pulled the extra pillow to my chest. Reece was handsome. Gorgeous, in fact. Obviously, I was attracted to him, men are visual creatures and he was very... pleasing, visually. And then add on that the whole life-and-death moment, I mean—who wouldn't want to fuck the guy that saved their life? All of that was just raw animal instinct. Things like the way he affected my body that were not remotely in my control. The way being close to him made my stomach quiver, the way his touch always spread warmth and reassurance through my body.

Intellectually, he was interesting, too. The way he talked was so unusual but earnest that it was endearing and easy to be amused at. It raised some questions, but maybe he was some kind of secret prince who grew up in a hoity-toity prep school before he became a...

A killer. I had to remind myself of that. Yes, in defense of me, but that only gave it context—it didn't change the thing itself. He'd killed two men. Made them dead. Disposed of the bodies, supposedly, too, which suggested that this *wasn't the first time.*

"What the fuck is wrong with me?" I asked the universe. It did not answer.

A metallic groan sounded from the opposite end of the cabin. Adrenaline flooded me, and I shot bolt upright and scrambled back to the corner of the bed, grasping for something hard or sharp around me and found nothing. My heart pounded, and all at once I was breathing hard.

I was alone. Probably it was the heat, playing over the outside of the camper, expanding metal that had finally had enough and had to stretch a bit. Still, my eyes dissected every corner, every shadow of the cabin, three or four times before I could unclench my stomach and scoot out of the corner.

My eyes burned. My belly churned and my chest constricted. A second later, my throat followed and I had to choke off a sob and close my eyes tight to keep from bawling.

I was shivering, I realized. Fucking pathetic. One god-damn sound, and it was like someone had pulled a trigger on a gun I didn't know was lodged in the base of my skull. I pulled my knees to my chest and wrapped my arms around them, and tried to stop looking for killers in my camper.

Some part of my brain, though, insisted that I could only be certain if I kept looking, and that sleep was completely out of the question.

I was at the table, having gotten stiff on the bed, when a polite knock at the door made my heart race again until it opened and Reece poked his head in from outside. He gave me one look and frowned. "You did not sleep."

"Couldn't," I said, and picked up a cup of coffee. "Caffeine instead. There's more, if you want some."

He sighed heavily and came into the camper, closing the door behind him. He must have been hot—I certainly was—because he cracked the windows on both sides before finally sitting down across from me. "What troubles you?"

"Is being targeted by an assassination squad not enough?" I asked.

Reece seemed to hold his breath. After a second, he exhaled slowly and nodded his head. "Of course it is. My apologies, it was not my wish to minimize your misfortune. I suppose after so many years, it is easy to forget how consequential such acts of violence can be."

I snorted, sipped my coffee, and searched his eyes for some sign of... anything, I guess. All there was there was naked sincerity, like there always was. "Why *do* you talk like that?"

His back straightened. "I don't understand the question."

"*It was not my wish to minimize your misfortune,*" I said in my best impression of him, which was probably lacking—I am terrible at impressions. "*I forget how consequential acts of violence can be.* You're like... from a play or something. You don't have an accent, you sound, you know, *American*, but nobody talks like that. Except maybe pretentious academics. But you aren't an academic. Are you?"

"That depends on one's definition, I think," he replied.

This time, there was a glint of something in those eyes that had more life than plain earnestness. I couldn't help smiling a little in response to it. "Now you're messing with me."

"Perhaps I jest," he admitted. "Only a little. I am… older than I appear."

"How old?" I asked. "Sixties?"

Reece pursed his lips and shrugged one shoulder.

My stomach quivered, almost as if there was something alive in it. Something shifting around, trying to get at him, or urging me to get at him one way or the other. It was such a distinct feeling that my hand moved to my stomach on reflex.

"Are you unwell?" Reece asked.

What would Yuri say? The thought came on its own. I could just imagine him politely excusing himself, giving me a wink, making some lewd gesture before leaving me alone with Reece.

I wasn't Yuri, of course. "This is going to sound… just so rude, potentially," I warned him. "It's none of my business, obviously, and you certainly don't owe me anything. I mean if anything, I owe *you*, you know? Um… but the thing is… I mean I'm just kind of wondering, like…"

Reece leaned forward ever so slightly, a crease appearing between his eyebrows. "Yes?"

The odd squirming in my belly got worse as nervousness made its way in alongside the other stuff, and I found that the words I wanted to say just wouldn't come out. My face grew hot and I leaned back in the chair. I waved a hand. "Never mind. It's not important. I'm just still in shock, I think, and my brain is doing crazy shit trying to make sense and cope and reach for comfort and it's stupid because it happened but it's over now, and I'm out here in the middle of nowhere without my phone, which should make it pretty much impossible to find me but somehow I still have this feeling like those people are right around some dark corner waiting for me and every time you're around me it's like that fear just kind of goes away for a bit and I'm projecting, I know, because I have a long history of doing that and…"

I realized I was out of breath, and sucked in air before I chuckled at myself and waved again. "Sorry."

Reece looked deeply concerned. He reached a hand out, palm up. I gingerly extended my own and placed it in his as if it might break. It felt *good*, and that rush of calm flooded me again.

After a few seconds of it, I was able to order my thoughts and words to match up. "Reece, do you like men?"

I felt the change in his body through his hand. Stiffness that froze him in place. I started to pull my hand away. "God, I'm sorry, I know that's not—"

But he reached to catch me as I pulled away, his fingers closing over mine. "You have not offended me, Matthew," he assured me softly.

"Good," I breathed. My mouth had gone dry. "Um… so is that like… never mind. You don't have to answer. It's none of my business."

"My sexuality," Reece said, "is… not as simple as you might be used to. It is not governed by constructs familiar to you, I suspect."

Well, I didn't have an answer to that. More weirdness from Reece, which was right in line with what I thought I knew about him so far. At least he was consistent. "Okay," I muttered. There was new intensity in his eyes. His nostrils were flared slightly, as well. A different kind of stiffness was in the set of his shoulders, in the way his knees were spread. Coiled, almost, like he might move at any moment. In someone else I might have thought they were about to hit me—I'd seen something like it before. But in him…

"So, then, are you attracted to… um, to me?" I barely got the words out.

Reece's jaw vibrated slightly when he opened his mouth to answer, and the breath that left him was ragged and shaky. "It would be a lie to say that I was not," he husked. "But… it is not such a simple matter for me as it may be for you."

"You're married," I said. "Is that it?"

"I am not mated, no."

I couldn't help a chuckle. "Mated. Okay. So does that mean you're single, or…?"

He let my hand go, with some apparent reluctance, and closed his eyes as he turned his head from me and exhaled a slow breath. The vein on the side of his neck throbbed. His heart was pounding faster than mine, it looked like.

Call it insanity. Call it a brief moment of boldness. Call it… almost being killed and feeling like I needed some confirmation of life because attempted assassinations are fucking stressful and afterward it turns out I needed some relief, if you want. Whatever it was that moved me, I slipped off of the chair, trembling, and met Reece's eyes as he opened them and watched me shift myself across the floor on my knees to get between his legs. He didn't stop me and I know that's not technically consent but it wasn't like he couldn't have, easily, as I slid my hands up the insides of his thighs.

"Matthew," he whispered, like a warning or a question—or both.

I reached for the buckle of his belt. "I just need a moment to not be afraid, Reece," I told him as I slipped my fingers under the leather to pull it free of the clasp. "Something to get in the way of these thoughts, all these emotions. If you don't—"

But he did want it. Or at least liked the idea of it. Because I could see his cock slowly filling out some of the material along his upper thigh. It pulsed as it swelled, until it was tenting against the cotton. I pulled the buckle open, and plucked at the clasp beneath, and tugged his zipper down. His hands remained on the table and the kitchenette counter respectively, and I kept my eyes on his for some sign that I should stop.

He only gave me a hard stare, the fine muscles of his face twitching at times, his eyes flicking from mine to my lips, to his straining cock, and back.

I hooked my fingers behind the band of his luxurious briefs, that were some kind of million-thread-count cotton maybe, and nervously pulled them away from the taut, tan skin of his waist. No tan lines were hidden there. I drew the soft material back slowly, waiting for the moment when he stopped me, called it off, put an end to it. I almost wanted him to, and I don't know why. There was something pulling at me that I couldn't explain, couldn't justify and didn't want to. Something that had gripped a part of me deep inside.

His cock sprang free, and a bead of clear fluid emerged from the tip. It throbbed, an extension of his beating pulse, a sign that I wasn't the only one nervous about what was happening, and the smell of him was something that made my mouth water. My ass clenched, my hole twitching with the strangest desire to have him inside me.

I leaned forward and pressed my lips to the base of his cock, kissing gently first there, and then further up as I squirmed forward between his thighs and slid my hands under his shirt. Every part of him was feverish, hotter than could possibly be safe, and it rushed into me, filling me up with every inch of him I explored with my fingers and lips.

He began to breathe hard enough that I could hear it. Deep, tortured breaths that I could feel in my hair even from so far away. That hot breath curled along my neck and even down my spine beneath my shirt, and when I finally reached the head of his dick, I looked up at him again and held his gaze as I licked the fluid that was now dribbling out of him.

The taste of it spread over my tongue. It was a strangely enticing kind of bitterness, like nothing I'd ever tasted. Miles away from any man I'd had in my mouth, and as it went down my throat it warmed me like good whiskey, smooth and earthy as it spread quiet fire into my stomach.

He didn't make any other sound until he dropped one hand to his cock and angled it toward my lips, and I slipped the head of him into my mouth. A low, rumbling growl came from him, vibrating his body so that I could feel it transferred through his dick and into my lips and tongue as I suckled more of his precum. My eyes fluttered closed, and I took more of him in, an inch at a time, wetting the hot skin with my tongue until I had him lodged at the back of my throat. I had never been much of a deep-throating type, and didn't embarrass myself by trying now, but the desire was there—to get as much of him inside me as I could manage.

I contented myself for the moment with just withdrawing at a snail's pace, exploring every subtle ridge of spongy, swollen tissue beneath the velvety skin with my tongue and lips. I sucked only enough that my cheeks added to what I hoped was a tight, wet tunnel, and was rewarded with another gush of precum when all that I had left was the thick head of him trapped between my lips.

My hand glided over his freshly wet shaft, twisting around the flared ridge of his cockhead to earn me another long, rumbling groan and this time a gentle hand that tangled in the hair on the back of my scalp. And more.

"Matthew…" He said my name this time like a whispered word of need, and I whimpered quietly as his hand urged me down again.

My hand grazed two looser patches of skin right at the base of his dick, and when I twisted it seemed as if the tissue underneath stirred. I bobbed slowly, and found that when I teased those two spots it seemed to make Reece's hips rock forward. He was gentle with me, never forcing me down, but seemed to want to get deeper inside with each slight thrust.

His breathing quickened, and his grunts and groans became more frequent. He muttered my name over and over again, each time with more urgency, and then his cock grew harder, the head swelling. I slid my other hand under the strained band of his briefs to curl my fingers around his heavy balls and felt them retracting slowly as he prepared to feed me what I now desperately wanted to get out of him. His fingers tightened around the fist of hair, and his other hand joined, resting lightly on the back of my neck at first, and then grasping and he held my head still and thrust slowly into me.

He held me there, his cock pressed to the back of my throat, as a shiver ran through him. I swirled my tongue, sucked harder, and moaned around his dick, trying to push him over, drink him down.

"Stop," he breathed.

I froze as I was, the tip of my tongue pressed against the swollen tube to milk out whatever I could get. He held me fast, and withdrew gradually. Something pricked at the back of my neck, startling me, and with the fistful of hair he pulled me off of his cock. It jumped once, and twice, and let loose a slow dribble of cloudy semen. I moved quickly to swipe it up with a finger before it spilled onto his pants, and stared up at him with open desire as I brought it to my mouth and tasted him.

Reece's jaw dropped in slow motion, his eyes unfocused one moment and rapt the next as I moaned quietly and savored the taste of him.

His posture took on that same coiled, taut look it had before, and the hand in my hair tightened, his arm barely twitching as if he would pull me into a fierce kiss.

My whole body was flushed with heat now, and as impossible as it sounds I could *sense* what he wanted in a visceral, wordless way that resonated in my bones, with not a shred of doubt to contravene it. He wanted *me*; to take me, get inside me, empty himself into me. And my body craved it in return, begging me to keep going, to fulfill some promise I didn't know was made until the prospect presented itself. The core of me ached to join with him.

"Please," I whispered. "Please, Reece. I want this. So badly, you don't know. Can you please? Just the once, even. I need you inside me. Need to feel… just, please. Take me, Reece. I'm begging."

My eyes burned, brimming with tears of frustration. All rationality had abandoned me, and I was raw, exposed.

"You don't know what you're asking," he said. "I can't… we shouldn't be…"

I grasped his cock, milked out another dribble of fluid, and strained against his hand to lap it up, begging like I was in heat. "Please," I muttered against the head of his dick, spreading his precum over my lips.

When he moved, it was with remarkable force. He stood, and hauled me to my feet with a firm hand under my shoulder. And then he was moving me toward the bed, the bulk of him an unstoppable force that I didn't dare even attempt to forestall. He snaked his hands beneath my ass and lifted me easily from the floor as we reached the bed, and laid me down on it as if I weighed nothing. His hands pawed at my shirt until I helped him take it off me, and then at my pants. The zipper tore in his hurry, and then with sure tugs he slipped them of me and threw them behind him. I reached for his shirt, but his hands caught my wrists and pinned them as he lowered himself onto me.

His lips pressed against mine, the vibration of a new, different growl spreading into my bones and turning them to liquid as I drank his kisses in. His tongue parted my lips, invaded my mouth and took over everything he found until I sucked helplessly at the strong muscle. His cock pressed to mine, and to my stomach, and I bucked my hips to grind against him before I spread my thighs and hooked my heels behind his flexing ass muscles. I pulled at him, trying to signal what I wanted. The churning in my stomach had turned gradually into a sweet kind of pain, like a hurricane of butterflies.

And nowhere in my mind was there any trace of fear. Just this. This hunger that commanded every muscle in my body.

I struggled under his rutting hips, trying to get his cock into position without the use of my hands. He continued to leak slick fluid, until my stomach was wet with it, and when there was enough I was able to make a final effort and his cock slid down the inside of my groin and brushed the cleft of my cheeks.

He breathed hard into my mouth and against my lips. "Matthew, I—"

"It's okay," I murmured as I reached down between us to angle him at my entrance. I gripped him loosely, but stroked up with my fingers to milk more of that prodigious fluid until it spilled down my crack, and used the head of his dick to spread it around my hole. I clenched and relaxed, massaging the thick head with my ring and opening myself slowly to him as his body seemed to push forward automatically.

It wasn't quite as comfortable as real lube would have been, but I was so turned on, so ready for it, that my hole relaxed by degrees and between the spit and his precum, the head of him popped through. I gasped, and winced against the brief pain, but when he started to pull back in concern I locked my heels behind his thighs and urge him forward. "I'm okay," I said. "I'm okay. Just go slow. Reece… come on, I want you inside. Please."

I swiveled my hips slowly as I begged him, and a look of tortured indecision crossed his face as he lifted it from mine. He searched my eyes as if looking for some secret, some indication that I didn't really want it from him, or maybe to a question I didn't even know yet. I lifted my head to brush my lips against his, though, and clawed at his back and hips to pull him into me.

And a bit at a time, he filled me. I'd been fucked before. I'd 'made love' before, plenty of times. I'd never had a man so tenderly and carefully thrust into me like this. Reece spread his knees, and slipped one arm beneath my back, the other under my neck. He cradled me close like this, and trapped my eyes with his as he exhaled slowly as he made his way inside me. My gland trembled with each inch of him, and I held my breath as he filled me, and could hardly force myself to take another breath until his hips were locked with my ass and he was as deep as it was possible to go.

I let out the breath in a wail, and pulled him close to me, burying his mouth against my neck where he didn't need me to ask that he bite me. He took a muscle there between his teeth and bit down with only enough force that it sent a shockwave of pleasure into my shoulder, down my chest, and right to the gland that his cock massaged as he hunched forward and back, thrusting with such precision that it seemed like we'd been doing this our entire lives.

With each thrust, I moved my hips to meet him, riding him from the bottom with mounting need. Heat poured off of him and I should have been sweating rivers in response but instead it passed through me, nested inside me, and turned every brush of his lips and teeth, every clench of his hands into my skin, every heave of his cock into my ass into an electric swell of ecstasy.

I didn't see my orgasm coming. There was no customary buildup. I plateaued, and then stayed there while Reece fucked me, until finally my body reached the limit of what it could take. It hit me with such surprise that I clawed my hands over his shirted back and heard fabric tearing. Every muscle seized, and at the very moment that hot, wet warmth gushed between our bodies as he crushed me to him and let out a roar that was not quite human as he slammed into me. His cock pulsed hard enough that I could feel it inside, and then warmth gushed through me as he emptied shot after shot into my insides.

And he kept swelling.

"Forgive me," he growled against my ear. "I can't…"

Something pressed against my prostate—some extra girth that was hard and sent an aftershock of post-orgasmic shivers clamoring up my spine. I arched my back as it struck me, and my cock spasmed again with a second, smaller but longer, lightning bolt of release. Every muscle moved on its own, and I writhed with the waves of pleasure as they cascaded up and down, lessening by degrees each time. It wasn't until they settled finally, that I realized the alien experience happening where our bodies were joined.

I started to move my hips to get him out of me, but Reece hissed and held me tighter—and besides that, I seemed to be… stuck.

A slender thread of fear wiggled into my stomach. "Fuck," I whimpered with mounting panic as I continued to gently tug my hips away despite Reece's efforts to hold me still. "Fuck, what is that?"

"I'm sorry," Reece breathed. "The way you smell, the way your body calls to mine. I should have been stronger, Matthew."

"What is happening, Reece?" I demanded. It wasn't an unpleasant sensation, and the more I moved, the more it rubbed against my gland, but it wasn't right—wasn't natural, and certainly should not have been happening.

"We're tied," he said. His body shuddered under my desperate embrace, and another bolt of heat entered me, the swollen part of his cock, I realized, flaring again to send a corresponding shudder of pleasure into me.

"Tied," I repeated. "What does that mean, 'tied'? What's happening?"

Reece gasped softly against my neck, and another gush of warmth filled me. "It means," he said raggedly, "that we've made a mistake. I've made a mistake. I'm sorry, Matthew. But… it seems… we are breeding."

Chapter 10
Reece

Never mind that the sacred omegas were believed to have gone extinct. My people were traditionalists, with laws of steel and fire that extended back hundreds of thousands of years. As another climax wracked my body and I expelled more seed into Matthew, my thoughts swirled to the consequences of breeding without permission, almost two hundred years before I was of age to even be considered. This would not go unpunished. It could not.

"Are you still…?" Matthew asked. His voice was weak now, his words raspy from a dry throat and wailing.

"Yes," I answered. My own voice was growing tired as well. "It will continue for some time."

He wriggled beneath me again, and in doing so tugged at my emerged knot that was lodged inside the tight passage of his ring. I keened softly against his neck and tried to keep him still as another bolt of fire spread up from my still boiling balls and leaked into him. "You must stop moving, Matthew."

"I know I said I wanted you in me," he breathed against my hair, "but I didn't mean permanently, Reece. Can't you… I don't know, pull out?"

"It would harm you," I told him. "We can only wait."

"How long?" he demanded.

"I do not know," I admitted. "Until it is finished."

"Breeding," he said. "Until the breeding is finished, is that what you mean? What the hell is going on? This isn't normal. It's the sort of thing you're supposed to mention. What do you mean by 'breeding'? God, are you some kind of… this is not… Reece, are you like an alien?"

With weak arms, I pushed myself up and off of him, to find his expression incredulous. "No," I said. "I am not… stars and moon, I—"

I was cut short when his muscles clenched around my knot. My eyes rolled, and my arms shook with the effort of holding me up as another orgasm stuttered through me. I knew that my kind sequestered themselves for the breeding ritual, but had never before considered that it was because of the vulnerability. Already, my body felt sapped. It was said to last days, in some cases. Foolish. What had I been thinking?

I had not been thinking. Clearly.

"Reece?" Matthew urged. "Please. I need you to answer me."

"You… you must try to relax," I rasped. "Do not squeeze like that. Remain still, I beg."

In answer, like some devious imp, he squeezed again. "Like that?"

I gasped, and my arms failed me as I collapsed onto him again and groaned through another wave of pleasure. "The… knot is very sensitive," I moaned.

He did not further assault me with pleasure, but he did gently shift himself beneath me until we were able to look at one another. "I'm very freaked out," he said calmly, though his eyes moved rapidly over my face. "And I need you to tell me what is happening."

"You deserve to know," I agreed. "It is hard to think like this. Forgive me."

"Focus," he urged. "Why is this happening?"

"I am not an 'alien'," I assured him. "But... I am not human either."

He stared at me, waiting, eyes wide.

"I am a dragon," I said.

Matthew's lips thinned as he pressed them together. The corners of his eyes crinkled. He squeezed again.

I clutched at his arm with one hand, and pulled him to me on instinct as I came again. Less intense—each time seemed to be weaker—but still enough that my mind was briefly blank.

"Dragon," Matthew echoed. "You can't expect me to believe that."

"I would prove it," I offered, "but there is not enough space here, and I fear you would not survive the change with me... inside you, as I am."

"Sure," he muttered. I opened my eyes with some effort, and saw a strange twinkle in his, his lips curled to a barely suppressed grin. "And this is how dragons do it?"

"As far as I know," I told him.

"As far as... wait, so are you like, a virgin dragon?" he asked.

There was no shame in it, but I bristled slightly nonetheless. From his tone, more than the words. "It is not so simple for my kind as copulating casually. There are rules. Traditions to be observed. One must be of age and..." I swallowed the words. Those traditions were pointless now, other than what they promised were we to be discovered.

Matthew groaned. "What do you mean 'of age'? Are you... fuck, are you like underage or something?"

"I am eight hundred and thirteen years old."

He laughed, and slid a hand up between us to cover his mouth. "I'm sorry," he muttered when it was past. "This is... it's really not funny, I just think I'm exhausted, and in shock and... this doesn't feel real? Like I'm about to wake up and wonder what the hell I ate that made me have a dream like this. I've been bred a few times, but never by a *dragon*, you know?"

"You have born children?"

My shock must have been evident on my face. Matthew's countenance changed from amused to pale with worry. "Um... no, Reece I haven't... I'm a man. You know that, right? Cock, balls, the whole nine... why would you ask me that?"

The full scope of my earlier words had not yet struck him. If I could have escaped to avoid this conversation, I might have done so. As it was, I was quite trapped. He squirmed again, uncomfortable the way we were splayed, and again my knot trembled with the threat of another release. I held him still with firm hands that did not have the strength to be successful. "Wait," I told him. "Let us… let me reposition us."

With care, I pushed myself up and got to my knees, then reached behind to swing one of his legs around to the front. It was a painful kind of ecstasy to turn his body and mine around, twisting his passage around my knot and still sensitive cock, until finally we could lay nestled together, his back to my chest. The clothes that I had not had the patience to remove felt more restrictive now, so I endured the tugging and squeezing and the accompanying jolts of weak orgasm in order to remove my trousers. With a bit more awkward struggling, I freed myself of my shirt as well, and pushed them to the side. The air was not cool on my skin, but it did relieve somewhat the stifling sense of restricted flesh.

"Good?" Matthew asked.

"Considerably better," I agreed.

"Talk," he said.

Certainly, he deserved to know what might lay in store for him. For both of us. "It is a long story," I warned him.

"How about the Cliff notes?"

"You… may not realize it," I said, measuring my words, "but you are one of some very few individuals that my people know as the sacred omegas. Your ancestors were gifted to mine after a tragedy befell our people. Our females were hunted and slain in an effort to destroy us in the long-term, even if in the short-term we won the battle against them."

"The Templars," Matthew whispered.

I nodded, and pulled him closer, if it was possible. An instinct had grown slowly in me, to somehow shelter him with my body, as if I could spread my wings and enfold us both. "Yes. They have been our ancient enemy for thousands of years. When they slew the last of our females, we were granted amnesty by the Wolven. The children of beasts and men, from days of old, who change their shape from one to the other. They had long borne children of both male and female. An artifact of their heritage. They took pity on us, and we ceded them territories where they might be safe from the cruelty of humans, and by way of exchange they gave to us seven omegas—young men, capable of bearing young. We mixed our magic with theirs, and took the shapes of men, and coupled with them. And so our people survived. The Templars sought to put an end to this as well, and so they struck again, and again, always seeking our concubines. Our generations are considerably longer than yours, you see, so… Matthew?"

He did not respond. I listened carefully, and held his body to mine to feel the gentle tide of his breathing, long and even as he slumbered.

I pressed my lips to the back of his head, gently so as not to wake him, and breathed in the scent of him. My long climax had slowed now to nothing but a weak tremble of satisfaction, ever present from the root of my cock to the top of my head, and I let my mate rest in my arms as I calmed my own thoughts. Perhaps, if I could sleep as well, we would wake uncoupled.

My mate. The thought came so easily. Dangerous, that. Perhaps my seed would not take. It had been generations since a sacred omega had borne a dragon's young. The magic might have waned, though the Ancients laid powerful enchantments. And I had not claimed him, though every instinct as I rutted inside Matthew's ravenous flesh had demanded that I do so. It was possible that we were yet safe from the wrath of my elders.

Only time would tell for sure.

Chapter 11
Matthew

I woke to the sound of someone pounding on the door, and the feeling of Reece's cock slipping out of me, and a quiver of pleasure as he did. That, and an urgent sort of fullness left behind that I had to clench against to keep from making a mess.

"Who is it?" I squawked in a groggy panic.

"Mercy," the intruder called. "It's lunchtime. Were all gathering at the mess tent. Um… you can join us if you want."

Reece rolled to his back as I sat up. "Be out in… a little bit. See you there, thanks!"

"Sure thing," she called back. I strained my ears to see if I could hear boots crunching away.

"You slept deeply," Reece rumbled from behind me.

I turned to look at him, still trying to judge whether I had dreamed everything. Maybe I had fallen asleep mid-fuck, but if so what kind of asshole kept going and then slept inside a person afterward? How was it even possible to stay like that through a long nap?

An urgent need assailed me before I could decide what I thought. Wordless, I slipped from the bed and strained to stay clenched as I scurried to the bathroom and drew the thin door closed. The last thing I wanted was this embarrassing moment after… whatever had happened… but there was no fighting it.

When it was finally done, and I was as clean as could be expected without a shower, I emerged to find Reece still naked but sitting up in the bed, a positively sheepish look on his face. "Are you…?"

I had an instinct to cover up, and crept back onto the bed, this time under the blanket so I could draw it up to my shoulders. We shared a wary look. I don't know what his was for, but I worried that if I said something, started this conversation, I'd have to look the madness straight in the face. My mind refused to accept what I thought I'd heard before I drifted off.

It couldn't quite square the sheer volume of… fluid… that I had expelled, though, either. I knew what hyperspermia was—a condition that produced excess amounts of semen—but it didn't explain… *that*.

"Are you real?" I finally asked. "I mean… you're not some kind of hallucination. Mercy and Professor Taylor, they didn't see me talking to myself or something? Because I feel like Mercy would just go with it and frankly Professor Taylor never struck me as particularly stable himself, so."

Reece's smile was forgiving, sympathetic, and twisted something in my chest. "I am real, Matthew."

"Okay," I said. Of course, that's what a person's hallucination would say, if they were thoroughly batshit insane, right? "Okay. So… what happened this morning, then… the way you, um…"

"Knotted," he provided. As if to help me understand, he spread his thighs and hefted his considerable cock so show the mounds of excess skin on either side. "It does not emerge all the time. When I pleasure myself, my body knows the difference. Only when copulating should it emerge."

"Yeah," I murmured, staring. How could I still be so thirsty for that? I shook it off and looked away. "Okay. So. You... knotted me... and you believe that there's some possibility that I'm potentially..."

He tilted his head slightly to one side. "With child?"

It was difficult to even hear it and not laugh. "Yes, that. And this is because I'm a sacred omega, and you're... you're a dragon. And the Templars want me dead because I can have your babies. Do I pretty much have all that?"

"That is an accurate summary," Reece agreed. He still had his cock in his hand.

"Can you...?" I cleared my throat and nodded toward his hand and dick.

He glanced down, took his hand away and used a pillow to cover up. "My sincerest apologies. I am unfamiliar with the instincts that currently drive me."

"Because you're an underage virgin dragon," I breathed. "I remember that part, too."

Reece's lips twitched, and he raised a finger as if to correct me. "I have copulated with humans before," he said. "I am not, in the strict sense, a virgin."

"But you are underage."

He sighed. "It is uncommon for my kind to breed before we reach our first millennium. It has been granted under particular circumstances, however, to dragons as young as five hundred."

"Well, I guess there's that," I said.

Silence descended. At least, between us. Inside, I was anything but.

"You should eat," he said at length. "We will not know for some time if my seed has taken—"

"If you knocked me up, you mean," I said.

Reece hung his head for a moment, before he raised it and nodded once. "As you say. I am very sorry, Matthew, that I did not say anything sooner. We believed your kind to be gone from the world. I did not realize the effect you would have on me, and was unprepared to resist it. To resist *you*. You cannot know the effect you have—there is a scent, and a pull at the very core of me, urging me on. To say nothing of the way you... ah. You are quite enticing, and skilled."

The laughter bubbled up out of me like a spring, and I couldn't hold it down. "Wow, so many firsts. No one's ever told me how enticing and skilled I was, Reece. Fuck me. Fuck. I... I can't even... Jesus. Let's just go get something to eat. I'm starving, and if I don't have some time to decompress I'm gonna crack right down the middle. Knocked up by an underage dragon..." I kept muttering to myself, very much like a crazy person, as I opened my suitcase and snatched out a pair of jeans and a tee-shirt and dressed.

Reece dressed as well, and together we emerged from the camper probably looking a lot like two people who just fucked. I was a little too distracted by the impossibility of it all to care, but there were definite glances from the rest of the dig crew as we entered the mess tent and gathered food from a small buffet that smelled good enough to be catered.

Mercy waved us down as we surveyed the three tables and their benches for a spot to eat. "Reece, Matt!"

Being as she was the only person I knew, and Professor Taylor was nowhere to be seen, we joined her.

"Feeling any better?" Mercy asked.

I frowned at her. "Sorry?"

"After a nap," she said, and waved her fork at Reece. "He said you needed rest. I figured you were sick, or just tired from traveling. You know I've got a piece of carnelian that can really get your energy flowing. Better than coffee, I swear."

It was an effort not to laugh. Then again, if Reece was a dragon and I could get pregnant, maybe a rock really was better than coffee. The world clearly no longer operated by familiar rules like physics or biology. "Maybe I'll take you up on that, Mercy. Thanks."

"Any time," she chirped. "I've got an extensive collection. And Mercury just came out of a nasty retrograde cycle so if you want to get your energies properly aligned, now is most definitely the time for it. You should come by my camper. Starting a big new project like this is the perfect time to relax, refocus your chakras, clear out old blockages..."

I tuned her out after that. If I had problems, I suspected that a few rocks weren't going to solve them. Reece seemed oddly focused on her, though, barely eating. Then again, did dragons eat canned ham, mashed potatoes, and frozen rolls? I tried to imagine a world were dragons existed. If they were as large as Taylor's supposed specimen, then they had to consume massive amounts of food. Did they breathe fire? If so, where did it even come from? And had Reece mentioned 'enchantment' at some point? Was he suggesting there was magic as well? Because that opened a whole other can of worms up and dumped them all over science.

I ate my food in silence—not Mercy's, just my own—and nodded or gave affirmative grunts to the multi-disciplinary-autodidact as she segued into an unfocused lecture about the positions of the planets when the dig was started and how they'd waited an extra day to start so that Mercury and Saturn would have a better relationship in some kind of election.

Lunch was called the old-fashioned way, with a work bell ringing from outside the tent. Everyone mustered their plates back to the buffet, where two of the workers started cleaning up. Mercy put together a plate and apologized for running off on us, but apparently, "Doc sometimes forgets to eat. Better go make sure he has something."

That left me and Reece, and little sense of organization. But we'd signed the papers and been given access. So it was time to take a look at this dragon skeleton. I wondered if Reece would know when he saw it whether it was real or not. Then if they were somehow related. I was trying to decide if that was a racist question to ask him, when Mercy returned to the lunch tent and flagged me down. "Ready to do some work? We've got some test results from the lab up north. You definitely want to see this. Come on!"

I smiled, and glanced at Reece. "Coming?"

He waved me on. "I will join you shortly. First, I believe I will look in on the dig."

Reece wasn't looking at me, though. He was looking at one of the workers. A dark-skinned, black-haired Latin-looking guy with bare arms and shoulders that would turn more than a few heads. Was that a stab of jealousy in my belly? No. I dismissed it. Silly. Obviously. "All right. I'll drop in after I see what Taylor's got. About time I took a look at this alleged dragon skeleton."

"Indeed," Reece murmured.

I followed Mercy out of the tent, and eyed the worker who was in a staring contest with Reece.

Why was nothing ever just simple and clear?

"So, Mercy," I said as we left them, "you said before that you're also a doula. That's like a midwife, right? Tell me about that…"

Chapter 12
Reece

When the other had gone, the worker with the aura of the beast about him strode forward, appraising me with a critical but cautious eye. I did the same, judging his gait, the set of his shoulders, and the careful way his boots crunched over the earth. Heel to toe, low to the ground, mindful of his balance. Just in case this was going to be a fight.

"You're in pack territory, you know," he said when he stopped just shy of arm's length from me, his hands relaxed, thumbs hooked loosely in his belt. "Not sure you're supposed to be here."

"I did not know," I replied, and waved toward the dig tent. "I understand there are people digging my kin up from your land."

He shrugged one shoulder. "She was buried here before the treaties. We have a story about it that my grandmother used to tell us."

"What story is that?" I asked.

He frowned, pensive. "You know, I can't remember the details. My generation stopped listening to the old stories. We prefer to make our own."

I took that as code that he didn't particularly care for ancient treaties. "Even so. I'm not actually here for the remains, or to make trouble with your pack. What's your name? My name is Reece."

"A dragon named Reece?" He asked. "I'm Joseph. Lopez."

"A Wolven named Joseph?" I echoed back at him.

His grin was feral and challenging. He knew that I couldn't risk shifting here. If he changed his skin, and no one saw him do it, it was just a strange occurrence for a big wolf to end up in south Texas sniffing around a dig site. If I changed my skin… well, one video recording would expose my people across the face of the Earth, from corner to corner. He had me at a disadvantage, though I was not helpless. I wanted very much to know, as far in advance as was possible, whether this seeming confrontation was intended to escalate.

But Joseph toned his challenging grin down to a friendly smile a moment before he offered his hand. "I'm Joseph Redpaws. I greet you, old one, and welcome you to the territory of the Pajalat Wolven."

We clasped our hands around one another's forearms. "Your hospitality is accepted, Joseph Redpaws of the Pajalat Wolven. I am Kestriatraverusinax."

I saw him counting syllables in his head, following my formal name. "Not so old as others, then," he said as he let my arm go. He stuck his hands in his pockets to show me he intended no harm. "There are two of your people south and east of here, near Mexico, you can't fit their names in a single breath."

I spread my hands. "We all are born, grow old, and die. I am fortunate to be far from the latter. Are there more of your people here? Did they know what was buried on their land?"

He shook his head. "Nah. We don't dig. What's in the ground ought to stay there, we figure. But, we heard there were white folks setting up camp. Worried they were going to build a mall, or an airport. You never know. Turns out they were digging, so I drew the short straw and signed up to keep an eye on things. I am sorry about it. Nothing we could do to stop it, though."

"The blame does not lie on your heads," I assured him. "Your people still keep the treaties."

Joseph bobbed his head amiably and gestured at the table where he took a seat. "My generation doesn't much care for some of the other stories," he said, "but they make damn sure we pay attention to the treaty codes. I don't know the last time one of yours actually set fire to a territory, but rumor has it that it happened a few times. Nobody wants that. That's, ah… not why you're here. Is it?"

I settled onto the bench on the other side of the table from him. "No. Truth be told, I did not know the nature of this dig. No, I came here with someone, hoping to take him out of harm's way. If I had known… I am not sure it would have altered the course of events so drastically, but I might have taken him elsewhere."

"The new kid," Joseph said. "Matthew Stiles, right? The paleontologist Doc used to teach."

Though I did not think Joseph was a threat, I could not help the ripple of protective anxiety that traveled through me at hearing his Matthew's name on a stranger's lips. I reassured myself that he had extended the pack's hospitality to me, and therefore to all under my charge. My experience with Wolven was limited, but they were said to be honorable above all else. "Yes," I confirmed. I glanced around the tent, and tuned my ears but neither heard nor saw evidence of onlookers or eavesdroppers. "Do you know who funds this project? Where the money comes from?"

"Me?" He laughed. "No, no. I'm just a grunt. I keep an eye open, an ear out, but they don't talk about where the money comes from. Not where I can hear, and I can hear a long way. Why?"

Not a threat, perhaps, but also not a trusted ally. "Only curious," I said. "It seems unusual, and of course I have an interest in anyone digging up the remains of my people."

"Welcome to our world," Joseph muttered.

He had me there, I supposed. I stood. "Do you mind showing me the dig?"

Joseph joined me and led me out of the mess tent to the dig site. The workers were back at it, squatting inside a deep pit sectioned by a grid of strings. They wielded brushes, trowels, and small picks as they carefully removed stone and soil. The pit was accessible either by ladder or, at one end, where steps had been carved into the wall and laid over with slats of wood. So far, not much of the dragon was exposed—only part of a skull, and the beginnings of two claws. Everywhere, there were stakes and platforms set up in the pit, presumably to keep unwary feet from crushing bone.

I didn't need to descend into the hole to get a clear look. From the snout alone, and the shape of the bones in the fingers, it was clear they were digging up the genuine article. "How long will the dig take?"

Joseph shrugged. "We can't fit more than six or seven down there at a time, there are ten of us and we work on a rotation. Doc wants to be careful, no damage, no scratching the bones by accident. He's thinking eight weeks to expose the top surfaces. But getting it all out… three to four months? I'm no expert. This work alone took five weeks but we had to dig the hole first and be careful. All sorts of equipment was set up first to take pictures with the sonar."

That seemed like enough time to make arrangements. The dig had to be stopped, of course. There was no question about that. The only real question was how to accomplish the thing without alerting the wrong people about why. Matthew would have some insight, I suspected. My eyes caught on a bit of bone with an orange tag tied to it. There was a perfectly round hole by the tag. "What is that?"

Joseph leaned past me to peer into the hole where I pointed. "Oh, that," he said. "Yeah, they took a core sample. You have to label any damage, that way later on no one wonders why the bones had this or that mark on them."

"A core sample," I repeated. "For analysis."

Joseph nodded.

"I think I should join Matthew and the professor now," I muttered, and left Joseph in the dig tent to see what the professor believed he had discovered.

Something told me that whatever it was, it was going to be a problem.

Chapter 13
Matthew

Professor Taylor was bent over a microscope when I joined him, trailing behind Mercy. His plate was untouched and still at his desk, the papers and folders he'd been studying arrayed around it as if he'd simply adjusted his organization to account for the new decoration. He looked up when the flap of the tent dropped closed behind us.

"Oh, Matthew." He beamed and waved me over. "Come, come. You should see this."

I stepped past Mercy and went to his microscope where he gestured for me to look for myself. I did, but although I recognized some kind of osseous slice of tissue I didn't know what exactly I was looking for. It was vaguely reptilian, and if Reece hadn't told me about himself I might have assumed it was from some remarkably preserved dinosaur remains. I took my eyes away from the scope. "Am I looking for something specific?"

Taylor licked his lips. "It's a bone sample. Look at the edges, at the bone matrix around the osteocyte. What do you see?"

I looked again. The matrix was thicker than usual, with a small hole where the osteocyte had once gone dormant after producing the tissue but...

He wasn't wrong, actually. There was something unusual. "Has the sample been contaminated?"

"No," Taylor whispered. "I took the sample myself, made the cross section, all in a clean box."

"It's possible there's been some kind of gradual leeching into the bone," I countered. "It's been underground for a long time."

"There are exotic mineral deposits in that sample, and in others," Taylor pressed. "It goes all the way down to the marrow."

It certainly looked that way. All around the edges of the thick, calcified shell there were flecks of darker material. In some places, it was clear that there were also small branches reaching out from one fleck to another, but with the sliver as thin as it was, it was impossible to tell if they actually touched. It reminded me of neurons.

I straightened from the microscope and frowned at Taylor. "When you say exotic...?"

He went to his desk and took a sheet of paper from one of the piles to hand to me. On it was a diagram of a cell like the one I'd seen, but there were lines arcing away from the flecks of mineral to make a complex network of lines that looked something like ripples on the surface of water. There were numbers below, readouts of some kind. I shook my head and waved the paper. "I don't understand this."

"The mineral deposits put off a magnetic field," he breathed. "But they're not ferrous. They don't react. And the electron microscope at the home office doesn't recognize it as a mineral native to our world."

I let that sink in, and heard my own voice asking Reece if he was an alien.

As if my thoughts had summoned him, he pushed through the flap of Taylor's tent. "Pardon my tardiness. What have I missed?"

Taylor snatched the paper from my hand and took it to Reece. He tapped the paper when Reece took it from him. "The bones," he said excitedly, "these are initial analysis notes about the structure of the bones. They're magnetic, and the mineral isn't on the periodic table. Can you believe it? Now you tell me, what kind of animal has bones like this?"

Reece examined the paper for a long time. I don't know if he even knew what he was looking at. All he was able to say, after almost a minute of searching the paper, was, "Fascinating indeed."

Professor Taylor spread his hands and turned to me, grinning like a madman. "You see? Can you see it? I was right!"

"It's still early," I said gently. "Let's just... get more of the skeleton out of the ground before we start publishing anything."

"But you can't immediately explain it away," Taylor pressed. "Right? It's new ground."

"I'll give you that," I agreed. Reece's eyes caught mine, and they did not look amused or happy. "Uh... but there's still the possibility it's simply a species of dinosaur we aren't familiar with. The mineral could be from a celestial body that contaminated the area. For all we know, it's that mineral that actually killed the animal, like a... cancer, or some radioactivity. We just shouldn't jump to conclusions until we've seen all the evidence. Right?"

"So," Taylor mused, smug as he glanced at Mercy, "I suppose that means you'll be sticking around?"

I was pretty sure there wasn't much of a choice in the matter, but Taylor didn't need to know that. I bobbed my head. "I'm definitely interested to see what we find."

Taylor couldn't have been happier than that. He clasped my shoulders in his hands, and then hugged me. "This will make us both famous," he murmured in my ear. "I'm so happy you could be here for this, my boy."

I extricated myself from him politely, and gave him as genuine a smile as I could. "No matter what we find, it's definitely exciting."

"Matthew," Reece said, the one word loaded with intent, "perhaps you should examine the dig?"

"I should," I agreed, and let Taylor get back to his work. Mercy held the tent flap open for us, and as we left I could hear her beginning to insist that Taylor take a break and eat something.

"So?" I asked. "What was that back there?"

"Until recently," Reece said, "the technology to examine our own biology in depth was not sufficient to—"

I stopped shy of the dig tent's entrance and waved at the mess tent. "No, I mean before. Who was that you had some kind of staring contest with?"

"Ah," Reece grunted. "That is not a conversation suitable to such an open area. We will speak of it elsewhere, in the camper perhaps."

He held the tent flap open for me, and waited.

There was no getting Reece to talk about anything he didn't want to talk about. I had a litany of questions ready for him the moment we were alone again though, and didn't intend to let him wiggle out of them for very long.

Most of those questions were temporarily forgotten when I stepped up to the edge of the massive hole and looked down at the emerging shape of the 'dragon' remains.

"Holy…"

"Yes," Reece said. "She was quite large."

"She?" I glanced up at him before staring at the skeleton again.

Reece shifted on his feet, and pointed to the bit of skull starting to show. "You can tell by the shape of her snout. The way it slopes at the end. For this family, it is common for the females to have gentle curves. The horns, which are as yet still hidden in the earth, will likewise display a longer, smoother curve. Males have a somewhat more shortened skull, with broad, thick bony plates above the eyes and horns that have a sharper forward curve. Like those of a bull, for an inept comparison."

I lowered my voice so that only he could hear me. "Do you have… horns?"

He nodded once. "They are quite shapely. I have received many compliments on them."

I suppressed a grin. "I see. When can I see them?"

Reece didn't answer right away, and when I looked up at him he only turned and left the tent. I stole another glance at the magnificent creature in the pit, and then followed him, hurrying to catch up as he walked toward our camper.

"Hey," I said as I fell into step beside him. "Did I say something wrong?"

"It is natural that you should wish to see my other form," he said softly. "But it is… not permitted."

I stepped in front of him as he reached for the handle to the camper door. "Not permitted? Isn't knocking me up also not permitted? Hey, look at me. You don't think maybe you owe me this? And a lot else besides. Like what this alleged pregnancy is going to entail? How long will it last, am I going to lay an egg?"

"You will give live birth," he sighed. "We are not birds, or reptiles."

"Uh, your bones say otherwise," I pointed out. "If I didn't know 'dragon' was an option, I would get something from the late Cretaceous period. Something big. How big are you? I mean, in your other 'form,' obviously."

Reece's jaw flexed. He looked away for a moment, out at the open desert beyond the camp before he gently pushed me aside from the door and opened it so that I could go in. I did, hoping he just didn't want to talk in the open.

"So?" I pressed when the door closed behind him. "Like, compared to another animal. Are you bigger than an elephant?"

His mouth twisted into a frown. "Considerably."

"Okay… bigger than a whale?"

"Larger than many," he muttered.

"Can you show me tonight?" I asked. "We could hike out into the desert a little bit, away from the lights."

Reece's lips grew thin, and he studied my face for some time. Finally, he sank into one of the chairs, pensive. "Let us wait," he said. "If indeed you carry my progeny inside you, then, I will reveal my true self to you. It is the way of things. Already, I may bear the judgment of one sin. I should not endanger us by committing another."

"How long before I know?" I asked. To me, it sounded like an excuse, a means to somehow drag this hoax out a bit longer. I tried to keep that out of my voice, but from the way he narrowed his eyes at me, I thought maybe I didn't do it very well.

"You will know in short order," he said. "Our progeny require considerable heat to gestate. Your body must change to accommodate the pregnancy. There will be some discomfort, but to what extent I cannot predict with certainty. I… have no accurate experience to draw on, only what little I have heard. Much of what comes is instinctual, though. Once, there was an order of midwives that served us. They were disbanded centuries ago. There may be written materials, but if so I do not know what has happened to them. Destroyed, most likely, to preserve our secrecy."

I folded my arms and leaned against the counter. "I can never tell if you're shitting me or not," I told him.

He raised an eyebrow. "Why would I defecate… this is an idiom."

"Uh… yes, it's an idiom, Reece." I shook my head slowly. "Everything you say sounds completely earnest, I can't even tell if you have a real sense of humor. If you were lying, I'd have no objective way to know."

"Why would I lie?" he asked.

I shrugged. "You're crazy? Some kind of narcissist with delusional personality traits? It wouldn't be the first time I'd attracted that kind of man. It's been kind of pattern with me."

"I did save you from assassins," he pointed out.

I snorted. "Those two things aren't somehow mutually exclusive."

"Perhaps not." At least he agreed with me on that point. But I wasn't sure if that was better or worse. He reached for me, and I couldn't quite help but reach back and let him take my hands. He pulled me gently to him, and gazed up at me. "I promised that I would protect you, Matthew. I spoke that oath in honesty, and I can assure you that my word is more than my bond. A dragon does not make any oath lightly."

"How would I know?" I asked.

Reece's eyes fell from my eyes to my stomach. He placed a hand there as if touching some holy relic that was forbidden, his hands shaking slightly. His palm was warm, and the touch so light that I wasn't certain he was actually pressing against me so much as hovering his hand just above my shirt. He swallowed, and looked back up at me with fierce eyes. "I will prove it to you," he said. "Because I know your nature; I can sense it with every part of me. And if, indeed, my seed has taken root within you, then you are the father of my child. The first dragon to be born in four hundred years. You are precious to me, and if it is required that I lay my life down so that you and our child may live then I would do so without hesitation and go to the Endless Sky joyfully, knowing that our family has survived."

Crazy person or not, my heart fluttered in my chest, pounding a little harder as my stomach trembled under his hand. I did *not* cry, because all of that was an insane person saying insane things but...

"I guess we'll see," I said finally.

Reece stood from the chair, and drew me to him. His lips grazed mine cautiously at first, and then pressed in with urgency. I let him, and then kissed him back when that heat filled me up like it had before. My knees lost a bit of stability, and his hands slid around my waist as if he knew I needed support to keep standing. It was a fierce kiss, something hungry and full of unspoken promises, and possessiveness that once would have scared me away—it was a red flag I had ignored more than once.

When he broke away, it was reluctantly. I had to catch my breath, and leaned my forehead against his chest to take lungfuls of air in slowly.

"I'll give you this," I murmured into his shirt, "you are one hell of a kisser."

"I have had eight hundred years to practice," he said.

I pulled back and looked up at him, half a grin pulling at my lips, to see the slightest sparkle of amusement glinting back at me although he didn't smile. "My God," I said. "You *do* make jokes."

"I make jokes all the time," he replied. "My culture is simply enamored of subtlety and depth."

With a sigh, I laid my head back on his chest. "And there it goes. I should get back to the dig and help out."

"It would be better if this project did not continue," Reece said as I pulled away and went to the door.

"I'll pitch that to Taylor and see how long he rants at me. Should be fun."

Reece put a hand on my arm, serious. "Matthew, I mean what I say. It seems that for the moment my people are unaware of what happens here. But if that were to change..."

He sounded worried. "What? What would they do?"

"To protect the secrecy that we now enjoy," he said gravely, his hand dropping from my arm as his eyes grew distant, "they would not be idle or at all subtle in action. They would see to it that this land was scorched to nothing. If they discover what we are about here, Matthew, and what you and I have done, the Templars will not be the greatest of our worries."

Reece was a hard man to read. Maybe he was crazy. Maybe his jokes were too subtle for my puny monkey brain to understand.

But the way he said *that,* I could tell plain as day—he wasn't joking at all.

He was afraid.

Chapter 14
Reece

There was no treatise written on the subject of pregnancy in sacred omegas. None that I had access to, in any case. However, it is often said of dragon mothers that as the ember of life caught fire within them, they became fiercer, even to the extent that their claws grew longer, their scales harder, their fire hotter.

As the days passed, I watched Matthew carefully, and inquired often as to his state of equilibrium—mentally, emotionally, and physically. Even the prospect that he carried my progeny within him triggered a latent instinct I had not known would show itself. My every thought became fixated on his well-being, and I began to interpret even minor inconveniences as potentially lethal threats. It became a struggle from moment to moment, to control my fire, my temper, and even at times my form. I craved the utility of my claws, tail, and teeth.

And I grew jealous. Perhaps only inhabiting a human body gave me the necessary rational mind to curtail this, but when we dined with the other humans I often found myself watching their faces, looking for any sign that they paid him undue attention that seemed more than merely professional in nature. He worked closely with Professor Taylor and Mercy, and there were moments when it became necessary to talk myself out of going to the tent to eavesdrop, as if Taylor were some rival male.

As little as was said about dragon mothers, even less was said of dragon fathers. Each day was a new, uncharted path through tangled skies with no obvious direction under my wings, so that I did not know if I was flying in circles or even plummeting toward the ground.

What I did know was that everything said about dragon mothers was very likely true, and seemed also to apply to sacred omegas who were with child.

"Does your abdomen ail you?" I asked Matthew, two weeks after I had tied with him, when we took our supper in the camper and he seemed uninterested in the food prepared by the crew. "If you find this unappetizing, perhaps I can travel to Catarina and—"

"Fucking Christ, Reece, I'm *fine*," Matthew snapped back. "I swear, if you ask me one more time… look, I'm just a little worn out, all right? It's hot out here and the hours are long and hardly any of the crew are professional so being in that pit is like watching toddlers pass around a Fabergé egg, and the future of my career is riding on this project one way or another so yeah, I'm a little stressed, okay? There's a lot of pressure and that's not even accounting for the Templars or angry dragons, so just give me some fucking space, okay?"

I judged it unhelpful to respond immediately with some reassurance that I only cared for his health. That course of action had only resulted in furthering his ire in the past.

All of it served to assure me, however, that he was indeed with child. I had not suggested this yet, but risked doing so now. There were preparations to begin making, if it were so. "Your demeanor suggests—"

Matthew leveled a glare at me that by rights should have burned me. "Don't. I'm stressed. That's all."

"If this is the case," I said, "perhaps you could allow me to assist in relaxing your body and mind."

"Like a massage?" he muttered, and picked at his food again.

"I speak of copulation," I said. "It seemed to calm you before."

Matthew convulsed, laughing unexpectedly. "That's got to be the most romantic invitation to sex I've ever heard."

Early on, I had difficulty discerning when he meant things literally, and when he was being facetious. Fortunately, I had acquired a great deal of practice identifying the latter in the past weeks. "I only wish to alleviate your discomfort."

He dropped his fork and pushed the plate away. "I can't eat this. One more day of packaged food and I'm going to start eating dirt. Actually… Jesus, am I really craving dirt?"

"Your cravings have changed?" I asked. "This is common to human pregnancies, is it not?"

Matthew eyed me. "So you know next to nothing about making dragon babies, but human pregnancy is one of your specialties now?"

I shook my head. "It is not. But I have taken occasion to speak with Mercy. Perhaps she can recommend a stone that would foster greater internal balance."

He pushed away from the table and stood, stretching his back as he did. "Don't get me started on Mercy's bullshit, please. I don't care how pretty it is, a rock isn't going to get rid of the headaches, or the heat, or my temperamental stomach."

"I understand that she is well versed in a variety of healing arts," I went on. "If you will not allow me to offer my assistance, then perhaps you can allow her. And the healing value of some stones was known to your ancient ancestors, among their other uses."

Matthew chuffed softly at that, and rolled his eyes—an expression he had mastered, I realized, with seemingly infinite degrees of subtle nuance that would fascinate even elder dragons. But, as he pressed his fists into his lower back, he considered. "I guess she does do herbal stuff as well," he conceded. "Maybe she's got some kind of tea or something. I know she's got a table. Some of the diggers go to her and everyone says she's pretty good at digging out knots. Maybe I'm just having trouble adjusting."

"Perhaps," I agreed. "You should see her, if only for the… for your own comfort." I had started to say for the health of the baby, but Matthew was not yet ready to accept that reality.

He did, however, respond quite well to unexpected and passionate displays of affection. I stood from the table, and placed his plate on the narrow kitchen counter. As I moved closer to him, and breathed in his scent, it was easy to produce a soft mating growl as I bent to kiss the side of his neck, just over his pulse.

"Are we going to try copulation then?" he asked, breathy as he leaned his head to one side, offering me more of his skin. His hands found my hips, and tugged me forward to press more firmly against him. "Because I didn't say *no*…"

I gave him the slightest nibble, just below his ear. Matthew groaned softly, but pulled away. When he did, he turned to face me. "But... I do feel like shit. Sorry. Maybe I should see Mercy. She couldn't possibly make me feel worse."

Perhaps it was nature, or perhaps it was more personal, but in either case I masked my disappointment. "I believe that would be a wise decision. If, afterward, you do feel better and desire my attentions... I will give them freely."

A slow smile broke over his face and he lifted himself up on his toes to kiss me. Heat rose in response, my fire stoked and spreading, reaching for him. But I held it in check as I savored the taste and scent of him. The desire to claim him properly nearly overwhelmed me. In claiming him, we might share more. Perhaps some of my strength would be his, and I might share a portion of his burden. That was the old way—to claim one's mate, to bond forever.

But whatever affection I felt for Matthew, whatever affection he felt for me, I reminded myself that it was in defiance of tradition and law. Were I to claim him, make him mine, and myself his—would ancient tradition protect us? Or would he simply suffer my fate with me?

"I'm gonna go," he breathed against my chin. "See if Mercy has some time for me."

"I will observe the perimeter," I told him as he brushed past me, his hand trailing over my stomach and hip.

He paused at the door. "Reece," he said, "let's say... let's imagine for a second that this is real and that I am pregnant and you're not crazy. What does that mean for us? I mean... are dragons like other lizards? Do you just make a baby and then wander off? Do I raise a kid on my own, or...?"

"As I have said before," I replied, "dragons are not lizards, Matthew. And no; we do not abandon our young. We devote ourselves to the well-being of our offspring, and to our mates. For life. To my people, nothing is more important than the bond between mates. It is sacred, and lasts beyond even death."

He nodded slowly as he rested his fingers on the door handle. "I like that," he said quietly. "It's nice. Romantic, even. I'll find you later."

He left me, and when he was gone I considered my own words. Nothing was more sacred to my people. So perhaps, if I claimed him, the ancients would have no choice but to accept our union.

Still... it was not a choice to make for Matthew, but with him. Any other way, and I could not hope that he would accept me.

Chapter 15
Matthew

"I'm so happy you asked for this," Mercy said as she scurried about her tent collecting stones in baskets. "I didn't want to say anything, but your energy has just been…" she waved a hand over her head. "Whoosh. Just out of whack. From like the day you got here. Probably it's this land. The energy of the dragon. It messes with everyone a little differently but you—well, anyway, just lie down here, face up."

I was hoping she would recommend some kind of shiatsu or something. Rub some pressure points. But now that I was in it, I didn't want to offend her. She'd jumped on the chance to try and make me feel better and who knew? Maybe her bullshit rock magic would at least be a nice placebo. Magic rocks were definitely pseudo-science, but I was confident in the reality of the placebo effect. So I lay down on her table and waited as she waved a variety of stones over my head until some mysterious process was completed and she placed one of them on my forehead, between my eyes.

"See, everyone thinks that a stone goes for each chakra," she said as she did the same over my throat, "but that's not actually right. It's individual. A personal kind of harmony that's unique to each person."

"People do like to jump to conclusions," I said.

She smiled, her eyes seeming wider behind her thick glasses as she looked down at me and carefully placed a bluish-looking stone at the hollow of my neck. "I know you don't believe in all this stuff."

I flushed a bit. "I… it's just outside of what I'm used to. That's all."

"I get it," she went said, plucking another stone from the basket to see if it 'harmonized' with my chest. "You're a scientist. Some things are hard to prove scientifically. After all, we can't even see the energy body with instruments yet. One day, maybe, if we look for it long enough. All I can say is, I've seen it work, I've felt it working. I'm a scientist too, you know, after my own fashion. I hypothesize, experiment, form a theory, work to disprove it, and repeat my experiments. I just have to accept that there are some parts of the data that are a little mysterious, and do the best I can. Oh—smoky quartz for the heart. You must have been through some stuff. Sorry about that."

I would have craned my head to look at her but didn't want to dislodge the rock on my forehead or throat. "Uh… what does that mean?"

More stones rattled in the basket. "Oh, well… smoky quartz is good for dislodging old patterns caused by pain. Trauma, that sort of thing. A good piece is mostly clear but had smoky inclusions, like it's been infected. When they're all used up, sometimes they break. But it's best to bury them before then, to send all that negative energy back into the earth. Hah—look at that, amber for the solar plexus. Independent much? I bet you're a little stubborn."

"I wasn't always," I murmured. "Dislodging old patterns, you said. Like… what's an example?"

She hummed thoughtfully. "I guess... I worked with a young lady about two years ago who had been in a really bad situation with a girlfriend. Abusive, it was terrible, but she'd ended the relationship and was trying to move on, get her energy realigned and centered on herself, you know?"

"Yeah," I said, though I didn't actually know what that was supposed to mean.

"Well, for her, it turned out that she was still looking for the same type of person," Mercy went on. "Hm. Not that one, okay. How about this one? No... Basically she was looking for all the same personality traits but hoping the abusiveness wouldn't be part of it. No surprise, she kept getting involved with abusive partners, ever since she broke it off. Because abusiveness, it turns out, is a personality trait. After a few weeks of sessions, she met this wonderful woman at a holistic convention in Sedona. They've been together ever since. They're even adopting children. Now that's funny."

"What?" I asked. She hadn't put another stone on me.

"None of these seem to jive with your sacral chakra. Mmm... let me get some others."

She moved away from the table, and a few more stones clacked as she gathered them. When she came back she tried two, and apparently neither of them were 'in tune' with my 'chakra'. The third one was the charm, though, and she laid it carefully there.

I was sure that the strange shiver that wound its way up into my stomach was just autosuggestion. Some kind of reward response for feeling like I finally met whatever expectation she had.

Mercy, though, made a curious sound of concern.

"How bad is it, doctor?" I joked.

Mercy didn't answer right away. She felt around my stomach, her fingers gentle. "It's, um... gosh, you know what? This is none of my business and I don't mean it the wrong way. If you identify as a man, then you're a man in my book, you know?"

"I am a man," I told her. "Biologically, I mean. I was born male."

"Oh, I know," she said quickly. "Trans men are men, you're born that way—"

"No," I grunted. "No, Mercy I'm saying I'm a cis-gendered male."

"Oh," she breathed relief. And then grunted confusion again. "Oh. Okay... it's just that the only time I've ever seen unakite harmonize with the sacral is, um... hah, you're gonna laugh. It's most common for pregnancy is the thing."

I sat up automatically. The stones on my body fell off and tumbled to the floor and table. Mercy looked very confused. "I'm sorry... why would you... what would make you say that?"

"Experience?" she offered. "But of course you're the exception. Maybe you're... pregnant metaphorically? Like with a new idea. Have you been deciding whether to write a book, or invent something?"

I realized I was breathing too fast. I took a deep breath and held it a moment longer, then lay back down. "Yeah," I said. "Yeah, I've been... thinking about getting something written. A story I had in mind. That must be it."

She replaced the stones, and made the same sound when she placed the unakite back on the lower part of my stomach. The next one went between my legs with a polite request that I lift my hips as she avoided touching my genitals. Others then went on my palms, at my feet, on my thighs, until I was more or less covered by rocks.

"The thing is," she said finally, when it seemed the last of them were placed, "unakite seems really specific. It's just strange. Maybe I need to rethink the unakite energy... because obviously you wouldn't be pregnant. Are you sure you aren't... I mean you're not intersex or something? Not that it's any of my business, I just—"

"I've only got the one set," I insisted. "Hey, you and Reece have spoken a few times, right?"

"Reece? Yeah, I've talked to him quite a bit. He seems really interested in midwifery. The mystery of birth—it definitely is something. I can see why he'd wonder."

I resisted the urge to move. "Um... he didn't put you up to the pregnancy thing, did he?"

Mercy moved into view, peering down at me with an utterly incredulous expression on her face. "What on Earth would he do a thing like that for? And why would I go along with it? Matt, I assure you I take this very seriously."

"Of course you do," I breathed. "Sorry. And I don't know why—he just likes to play practical jokes."

"He does?" She snorted and shook her head as she pulled back out of view. "Funny; he doesn't seem the type at *all*. Guess you never can tell about people."

"No," I said. "I guess you can't. Uh, how long to I stay like this?"

She stood at the table and grinned down at me. "Until you feel better!"

I couldn't shake what Mercy said to me as I made my way through the camp looking for Reece. It wasn't dinnertime yet, but he wasn't in the dig tent or with Taylor, and he wasn't in the camper. He had said something about the perimeter, so maybe he was patrolling. Looking for signs of imminent Templar attacks—whatever that looked like.

When I couldn't find him, I went to the dig instead, but my lower back was already killing me from four hours that morning spent squatting and hunched over a section of tail vertebrae that were just beginning to emerge from the soil, and from climbing up and down the steps with buckets of loose dirt to move out of the pit.

Still, I watched the progress, and tried to match up what I was seeing now with the sonar image Taylor had showed me. It seemed to match, which ruled out—or at least, suggested ruling out—that the image itself was the hoax.

Although I had entertained the notion before, I revisited the idea now that maybe this was all real. That was a dragon skeleton, Reece was himself a living dragon in human form, there really were Templars out to get me and, presumably, him as well. Maybe Mercy's rocks really could tell her that I was pregnant.

Maybe I really was pregnant.

My hand moved to my stomach. Could I sense the beginnings of a child in there? Was there some subtle feeling of new organs moving into place? How would it even work? Reece had mentioned enchantments and magic before—was that what would happen inside me? Some kind of magic would rearrange my insides to make way for a fetus?

Suddenly I couldn't decide if I should have paid more attention in sex ed, or if it wouldn't have done me any good to begin with.

"Everything okay, Mr. Stiles?" A voice asked from behind me.

I turned to see Joseph returning with a bucket. We'd worked on some of the same sections together, and I liked him well enough. He was talkative, but not especially intellectual—or at least, he preferred to talk about mundane things while he dug. Music, movies, life in rural Texas. I stepped out of his way. "Yeah, I'm fine. Just a little... I just got back from seeing Mercy. And I told you, Joseph—call me Matt, please."

He grinned wide. "Oh, she got her voodoo on you, huh?"

"I don't think it was specifically voodoo," I chuckled. "But yeah, basically."

"Feel any better?" he asked.

My back still hurt. But other than that... "You know I think I actually do. Probably just from getting a little rest in the middle of the day. Not ready to blame magic rocks just yet. Funny thing, you know, she thinks I could be pregnant. So."

Instead of laughing at that, Joseph's smile froze. "Pregnant. Huh. Who would the father be? Besides you, I guess. Reece?"

I frowned. "Joseph, obviously I'm not... why Reece? Just because we sleep in the same camper? He's my natural history consultant, we don't—"

Joseph leaned in. "You know these campers aren't like, soundproof, right?"

He tilted his head a bit, then glanced outside the tent through the flap. "Hey, speak of the devil. Here's your consultant now."

A moment later, Reece poked his head in through the opening. He nodded to Joseph. "Joseph."

"Reece," Joseph returned. "I guess congratulations are in order."

Reece blinked. "For what?"

"I'll let Mr. Stile—Matt, I mean—tell you," he took the bucket to the edge of the dig hole and passed it down before he crawled down the ladder to resume his work.

Reece pinched his eyebrows, and started to ask but I waved him out of the tent and joined him outside. We walked some distance, outside the ring of campers before I said anything. Even then, I had to pace for a moment.

"So," I said, "I saw Mercy. And I do feel a little better. But something really strange happened."

I told him about it, about the stone and what Mercy said. And then added in Joseph's reaction for good measure.

"Did you say *anything* to Mercy about me being possibly pregnant? Or even like... make a joke about it or something? Apparently everyone in camp knows we've been fucking."

"You are not quiet when we copulate," Reece explained, but quickly moved on before I could comment, "and no; I said nothing to Mercy regarding pregnancy. It is a conclusion she must have come to on her own. She seemed certain?"

"No," I said, "she seemed confused. But... I don't know why she would have said it unless..."

Reece finished the thought as he put his hands on my shoulders and gazed at my stomach in open wonder that I hadn't seen him display before. "Unless by some faculty she possesses, she was indeed able to discern for herself that you carry my child."

"Reece," I said quietly, placing my hands on his. "Reece, I'm... really starting to freak out. What do I do?"

He pulled me into a kiss, and held me tight for a long moment. When he released me, there were thin streamers of *vapor* around his eyes.

"What *we* do," he said, "is shepherd a precious life into this world. Together. My seed grows roots within you. A new dragon shall swell your belly. You do not know what an event this is, my mate. It is joyous. It is a miracle."

"This can't—"

He pressed a finger to my lips. "I understand," he said softly. "It is new, and seems impossible. Tonight... I will show you what you wish to see. When the sun sets, we will go beyond the light of the camp. There, I will reveal my true nature to you. Then you may decide for yourself what is real."

Much as I wanted to see that—to know for sure that he wasn't just pulling some elaborate trick—something told me that if he really did reveal to me that all of this was real... it wasn't going to make anything better.

It would just make it all dangerously real.

Chapter 16
Reece

The day wore on longer than I expected. It was difficult to discern whether it was worry or excitement that stretched time and slowed the sun's path through the sky, but either would have been as appropriate.

Centuries ago, when the bloodlines of the sacred omegas were carefully watched and recorded, the moment of revelation would come before the mating. A dragon, given the blessing of the ancients to breed, would court the omega selected for them with art, and poetry, and performance. They would woo their intended until their solicitation was accepted. Then before mating, the dragon would reveal himself to the sacred omega. It was a moment of truth, and trust, and good faith.

Since the final blow of the Templars four centuries before, no dragon had revealed himself to a human. It was forbidden. Those that did were, like Tarin, declared to be outcasts and forbidden from even passing through another dragon's territory. It made travel nearly impossible, and more importantly it deprived one of my kind from the company of the only beings on Earth that could be called peers.

That night, I would break yet another law. My fate was all but assured.

Fear, yes. That Matthew might turn away from me. That my actions would be discovered and my punishment compounded. For such violations, I could be more than outcast. I could be committed forever to the flesh of a mortal, to live and die in the space of a breath, to never again feel the wind under my wings or the true extent of my fire.

Excitement, though, as well. To finally reveal myself to my mate. To allow him the rare treasure of knowing beyond a doubt that such beings as myself existed, to open his eyes to magic that he did not yet imagine. Matthew's very nature was curiosity, exploration, to seek answers and uncover truths. If he did not run screaming at the sight of me, then perhaps as my brethren in the past had experienced, I would see wonder and elation in his eyes.

It was a gamble. But so had all of this been.

As slow as it was, time cannot but pass. Bit by bit the sand of the hourglass passed us, and in time the sun relented and went to its rest.

After supper, Matthew and Mercy exchanged some short words about his well-being, and Taylor asked that Matthew be available to procure and process new samples from the remains. Joseph avoided us, but gave a meaningful look. Matthew had told him about his alleged 'pregnancy' expecting the Wolven would laugh off the very idea of it—because he did not know Joseph's nature and I had not told him of it. Rather, Joseph was as concerned as I, I thought. We dragons were not the only beings to have believed the sacred omegas were gone from the world.

When all was done, we retired to our camper. "We should wait until all are sleeping," I suggested.

Matthew lifted an eyebrow, as he so often did when I spoke. "You planning to chicken out on me? Stars aligned wrong, or can you only change on the witching hour?"

"I was not aware there was an hour set aside for witchcraft," I shot back. "Would that hour be relative to one's place on the globe, or is it one hour in each day shared by all practitioners?"

He looked uncertain.

"I was making a jest," I said.

Matthew huffed a single laugh, and shook his head as he wandered to the bed and sat down on the edge of it, his hands folded in his lap. "Dragon humor is very dry."

"We are creatures of fire."

This time he laughed more genuinely, and the sound of it relaxed me somewhat. I approached him as I took my jacket off and laid it on the table.

"Do you have other clothes?" he asked, gesturing at the garment. "How do you keep your one shirt so clean?"

"It is not precisely real," I said. "A... byproduct of the change. Every other night, I go out into the darkness and change, so that my true eyes may pierce the darkness. In my true form, I can see a great distance with clarity. These eyes are insufficient to protect you." I tapped at the corner of my left eye and then shrugged as I dropped my hand and closed the rest of the distance until I was standing over him, only a foot away. Close enough to touch. "When I return to this form, I incorporate the clothing as well."

"I have to admit," he mused, "between that thing you do with your, um... well, the thing where we get stuck together, and the magical laundry, you've got some impressive tricks."

My cock stirred at the mention of the knotting. "It is not so much a thing I do as a thing that happens."

"Either way," he said. His eyes dropped briefly, and then turned away. "Doesn't take much, does it?"

"What?"

He bit his lip and ran a hand up my thigh until he reached my swell. His fingers only barely brushed it before he took his hand away. "Sorry."

I cocked my head to one side, and then leaned in to take his hand and place it firmly there. Under his palm, I grew harder, and with my free hand I tilted his chin up. "You need not apologize. You are my mate, Matthew, intentionally or not. I have only a three priorities now. To guard you, to provide for you, and to be at your disposal. I am, in whole and in parts, yours entirely. If you wish for me to—"

He withdrew his hand, and climbed back onto the bed. Not to entice me, I thought, but to create distance. He pulled a pillow into his lap and drew his legs under it to sit cross-legged. "If I wish for you to what? Tend my needs?"

"Yes," I said simply. "Whatever needs there are, it is my obligation... does that not please you?"

Matthew hung his head, and begun to shake it. When he looked up, he seemed sad. "Sometimes, Reece, I think you must really want me. That you get hot for me. Then other times it seems like it's only when it looks like I need to be kissed or fucked that you're interested. All this talk of dedication, and obligation, and being your mate—whatever that means beyond my being..." he sighed, and waved a hand to dismiss it. "I don't know, maybe it doesn't matter. I'm not even sure a dragon would understand; for all I know your culture is predicated on a reptilian sensibility. Or something akin to it—I know, I know, you're not a lizard. Not really. Still, do your people feel things like love?"

"Do yours?" I asked.

He screwed his face up. "Are you kidding me? Humans are idiots for love. We start and end wars for it, we die for it, we... get so fucking tangled up in it that we can't see straight and make terrible decisions and alienate everyone we know and throw away our futures. Yeah, we're capable of love. Like, way too much, maybe. Even when it doesn't make sense."

There was desperation in his voice. He wanted something from me. Eight hundred years of walking among humans, watching them, but staying distant from them with only some few and rare exceptions—I had never had occasion to consider the nature of their love. Or to compare it with my own.

"My people... live long lives," I said as I slipped onto the bed. "Among humans, love is so intense, perhaps, because your lives are so brief. All experiences must be precious. To us, love is different. It is not lust, or a compulsion to pair and breed. Even breeding is calculated, regulated. Love to us is duty, honor, tradition."

"So it's not emotional," Matthew muttered. "You don't have an emotion for it. Something that drives you."

"I feel considerable emotion for you, Matthew," I assured him. "Since we coupled, and even before, I have had a strong compulsion to see that you are safe, and that our child is safe. I have told you, I would lay down my life—"

"But do you *love* me, Reece? And can you?"

"Do you want me to?" I asked.

He groaned and rolled his head back to thump it against the wall of the camper. "See, if I say yes, and then you act like you do, I'll always wonder if you're just putting me on. If I say no, and you act like you don't because you don't think I need that, then I'll be bitter and disappointed because you don't. It's a catch twenty-two."

Humans could be hellishly confusing.

"Perhaps I cannot answer you now," I said. "I will not lie to you, Matthew. We are not the same, you and I. Not truly. Come. Let me hold you."

"Why?" he asked. "To make me feel more secure? To do that thing you do that gets into my head?"

"Not your head," I said gently as I tugged at his arm. "Your heart. Your spirit. But I will not do that now, if you prefer it. I only want to be close to you. To feel your body against mine, to hear the beating of your heart. To comfort you, and take comfort in you. Now while I have the chance. Soon, I fear, you will not wish to look on me."

Matthew's features softened. He bit his lip as before, and wriggled over the bed to me, into my arms, where he nuzzled against my chest. "Maybe… maybe we just have different words for things."

"Your tongue is rudimentary and young—"

"Reece," Matthew breathed, and pulled my arms tighter around him, "stop talking."

Chapter 17
Matthew

I dozed off against Reece's chest, but didn't realize it until he nudged me gently. "It is time to wake, Matthew."

Bleary-eyed, I checked that I hadn't drooled on him and let him help me sit up. "I fell asleep," I muttered.

Reece brushed his knuckles over my cheek. "Indeed, you did. Do you feel rested?"

"Don't know if I would say that," I said. "Did you? Never mind. I'm betting you only sleep once every hundred years or something but it's for like months at a time. Right?"

"I slept the morning that we copulated," he said. There was a pause, and he shrugged. "But that was something of a special case. Normally I sleep for approximately three days, every few years. I do rest between, however."

I leaned back on the bed. "Do dragons dream when they sleep?"

"All beings dream," Reece said. "There is only one person in the camp awake. I believe it is Professor Taylor, and I do not believe he is able to spare attention to anything beyond his tent. If you are ready, we should go now."

"Right," I hesitated as I swung my legs off the bed. "Can you hear all of that?"

Reece nodded. And he had the kind of smile that I could almost call a smirk.

I grunted at that, and trusted his word. Besides—either we'd go out into the desert and he'd have nothing to show me, and it didn't matter if anyone was awake; or he'd do as he promised, turn into a dragon, and I would have far bigger worries than whether anyone saw us. "Then let's go."

I had to wear both a sweater and a heavier jacket for the walk. The sun was brutal during the day, but the desert night got its say in the end. It had to be near thirty degrees. Reece stayed close to me, one arm over my shoulder as he guided me over a landscape too dark for my eyes to easily adjust. Several times, he warned me about a bush or a hole in the ground that I couldn't have seen if I was on my stomach and staring at it. The stars gave off weak light, but the moon was down to a final sliver of fingernail before it took a couple of days off to rest in the shadow of the Earth.

When we'd walked for what seemed like an hour, Reece finally stopped us, turned to look back at the far-off twinkle that was the campsite, and declared that we were far enough away.

I tried to see more clearly by sheer force of will. "Well, if you did it here, I'll probably never be sure about what I saw. Smart strategy."

"You will be able to see," Reece assured me. "I will see to it."

"Gonna breathe some fire?" I nudged him with my elbow.

"That would be ill advised," he said. "Remain in this spot. I require some space. When the change occurs, I beg you—do not flee. It is dark, and you may harm yourself."

I crossed my heart. "Promise. This should be good."

He bent his neck to kiss me, and let my hand fall from his. "I would never harm you, Matthew."

All I could muster was a nod. Now that we had arrived, now that it was about to happen—or not happen—my stomach was bound in a tight knot. Two utterly incompatible expectations warred in my mind. Either this was all real, and the world that I knew was magnificently incomplete, or this was the end of the joke and I had begun to fall for a yet another sociopathic narcissist.

Please turn into a dragon, I prayed.

Reece left me, and disappeared in the darkness. I heard his shoes crunch in a night that was mostly silent except for a brief call of distant coyotes. It wasn't safe to be out this time of night on my own. I might have grown up in the city, but I knew that much about the country. I wasn't the top of the food chain that very moment.

Something in the air changed. It was a warm breeze, out of place in the desert air, and the vast, empty night changed shape to my ears—as if a mountain had silently emerged in front of me, changing the way even my breath sounded.

I swallowed hard, as a primal, instinctive kind of fear crept up my spine and closed a hand over the back of my head so cold it made the night seem tropical. "R-Reece?"

A voice emerged from the darkness. Deeper and bigger than Reece's, the kind of base I could feel through the ground. "I am here, Matthew. Do not be afraid."

Something moved toward me. Something massive. The parched earth cracked and crunched before me, and then some massive animal chuffed in the darkness. A second later, the tiniest spark of light appeared in the air, rose up, and gradually grew brighter until I could see what was hidden in the night.

Every muscle in my body screamed for me to turn and run. "H-holy… fuck."

Even if I had believed Reece wholeheartedly from the moment he told me what he was, I couldn't have imagine *this*. A saurian head loomed over me in the darkness, a scaled face decorated with curved conical horns that followed ridges defining a sloping, graceful snout, like a T-rex with horns and a wider skull. The light caught the dragon's eyes and made them flash gold and copper.

It was the size of a Volkswagen beetle.

A long, thick neck led to a much larger body, and as my eyes traveled over the broad scales, Reece spread his wings slowly at first, until at the last moment they snapped the final distance with a crack and he reared back on his hind legs to put himself on full display. His form was muscular, towering, and utterly terrifying to the part of my brain that remembered being prey in some ancient jungle.

Reece lowered himself back to his forelegs, and dipped his head toward me until the tip of his nose barely grazed my knees. I had to remember to breathe. When he nudged my legs gently, careful not to bowl me over, and chuffed hot air over my legs, I took a step back involuntarily.

The dragon's eyes angled up at me. "I beg you, my mate. Do not fear me. I could no more harm you than pluck the sun and moon from the sky."

He lifted his head just enough that the crest of his snout was within easy reach. Breathless and trembling, I took the invitation and reached out an unsteady hand until the very tips of my fingers brushed warm, smooth scales. The night chill had gone, chased away by the heat this creature created, as if there were an inferno burning somewhere inside him, barely contained.

"You're... warm," I said.

Reece made a deep, thrumming sound in his chest, like the slow rattling of a mountain. "I am a creature born of fire."

"Okay." Slowly, the world turned sideways, toppling over until I lost my balance and stumbled. Quicker than I would have thought possible, a great taloned hand caught me, steadied me, and stayed in contact with my hip until I regained my footing. "So it's all real then. Isn't it? Templars, and dragons. The dig... and if that's true then... then I'm really..."

Reece's nose nudged at my belly affectionately. Another Richter scale-registered rumble came from him, rhythmic and sustained this time, even as he spoke. "You carry my hatchling inside you," he confirmed. "And more—the future of my people. There are so few of us, Matthew. And perhaps there is only one of you in all the world. I do not know. But I know that you are precious to me, beyond all else."

The throbbing, rolling sound from Reece's chest seemed to seep into me, calming me, and allowing other emotions to be heard over the fear.

"You're a fucking dragon," I gasped, slowly smiling at the sheer magic of it. I chuckled then as my ears finally made sense of that noise he was making. "Are you... Reece, are you purring?"

He huffed out another hot breath, tickling my stomach through my shirt, and turned his head sideways at me like a bird, cocking it a few degrees down to eye me. "Dragons," he said, "do not purr, Matthew."

I licked my lips and reached out again to explore the ridges over an eye as large as two dinner plates. The muscles beneath rippled as if ticklish. There were great horns along his back as well, all swept backward, and a pair of bull-like horns at the top of his head that swept forward and looked dangerously sharp. Nothing about him seemed aerodynamic. "Can you fly?"

"I can," he affirmed. "At great heights and for many days if needed."

"Could I ride you?" I asked.

There was no way to call myself an expert on dragon facial expressions or body language after just five minutes with one in the dark, but I took Reece's suddenly half-lidded eye to be something like offense or disapproval. The corner ridged saurian lip, however, curled as he parted his mouth an inch. "Wait for me here."

The light above us dimmed to almost nothing, leaving the world barely lit again as he withdrew into the dark. There was a faint shimmer, barely visible to my eyes—I could have imagined it, I decided—and again the content of the air changed. Reece's tall, broad silhouette, human again, emerged slowly as he crunched his way toward me.

Naked.

He stopped inches from me, and tipped my chin up. His kiss was fire, like him, and spread through me, wrapped around me, and filled me with need. "I cannot take you to the sky," he murmured. "The air is cold and thin, and I would not endanger you. But that does not mean you cannot ride—as often and as long as you desire."

As he pushed my coat off my shoulders, and curled his fingers under the edge of my shirt to take it off me, and I felt the hard lines of his body pressed against mine, I reached between us to wrap my fingers around his cock. It was already hard, and pulsing against my palm. "I do desire," I whispered into his mouth. "Often and long."

Reece purred again, and slid his hand down the back of my pants to grip one ass cheek in his great paw-like hand. "As you wish, my mate."

Chapter 18
Reece

Matthew's body melted against mine as I crushed him to me, his mouth yielding to my tongue and lips as I indulged the hunger that demanded sating. The scent of him enveloped me, invaded me, and sank hooks deep into my body and soul. *My mate*, they told me, again and again as I tasted him, and demanded that I mark him as my own, claim him and bind our lives together.

The effort of resisting, and forever dooming him to whatever fate awaited me, was a physical one. It coursed through me as I clutched at the smooth, soft flesh of his cheeks, as his hand pumped my rigid cock until I leaked into his hand and made it slick. It was in every inch of me, clawing at me from the inside as he tore himself from my mouth and sank to his knees. The desire grew so powerful that when his wet lips caught the head of my weeping dick between them, I grabbed handfuls of his hair and roared at the night sky as he devoured me.

His hand glided along my shaft, slick with both of us, and every flick and sweep of his tongue shook me like a man struck by lightning and thunder. It was loss and victory to be consumed by him, a funeral dirge to hear the soft moaning and feel his mouth vibrating around me gently. I gazed down at him, my eyes shifted just enough to see him so that I could drink in the sight of his knit eyebrows as he sucked me down.

"Matthew," I crooned at him, "slowly, my sweet. You will end me."

His eyes opened just long enough to glance up at me in the dark, and the corners of his mouth twitched up before he wrapped them more firmly and sucked harder, his grip tightening so that the ridge of my cock head popped through his fingers and was forced through a tight ring when he took me in again. Each exquisite plunge threatened to ruin me, every withdrawal the promise of an endless torture. His soft moans grew urgent, pleading, as he bobbed his head, and the fingers of his other hand caressed the delicate skin covering my knot. The flesh there flared, swelled, and relaxed as he explored, and finally he discovered that if he massaged firmly there with the tips of his fingers, it caused my knees to shake and bent me over him as I gasped and panted and endured the exquisite agony of it only because he seemed to so love what he could do to me.

Too soon, my balls began to churn and tighten. I held my breath, every muscle locking as the slow rhythm of his mouth and the subtle sound of suckling transfixed me. "Matthew, I'm…"

I didn't finish. Words turned to motes of ash in my mind, and he closed a hand tight around my half-swollen knot just as my cock stiffened and small muscles twisted tight inside. A second later I was falling in slow motion to the ground, my knees unable to support me longer, as Matthew chased me down and drank the fiery seed that gushed out of me and into his throat. He made delighted sounds between swallows, and began to struggle between swallowing and laughing by the time the seventh or eighth spasm struck me and fed him more.

By the time he finished, I was shaking, my eyes half-lidded, my body jerking involuntarily as he teased my sensitive cock head and massaged my faltering knot. The electric pleasure of it was almost too much to bear, but I dared not stop him and break the spell in the moment.

He stopped on his own after an eternity of teasing, and kissed me. The mix of his breath and my seed was on his tongue and lips, and however spent I was, it seemed my energy had simply been taken from me and stored somewhere inside him. His body wriggled and squirmed against me until I wrapped him in my arms and fell back against the rough ground. I barely noticed the poking of small stones and brush at my human body—it was a transient annoyance, and one that I bore with pleasure if it meant sparing my mate the discomfort.

Matthew nibbled at my lower lip, and rocked his hips against mine, hard in his trousers. "You're still hard."

"Far from spent," I said. "We could go back to the camper—"

"No," he breathed as he reached between us and unbuttoned himself. The zipper followed. "I like it out here. In the open air, in the wild. You taste incredible. I already want more."

I chuckled as I grabbed his hips and helped lift him up so that he could divest himself of what clothing was left. "All that I am is yours. If it is my seed you want, you may have all of it."

When he kicked his trousers off into the darkness, he crawled up my body, straddling me so that his knees must have scraped on the earth. "I want all of it then," he mused as he bent to kiss me, and reached behind him to squeeze my cock, breathing in the sigh of pleasure I gave at having his hand on me again. "But I want the other thing, too. The… you know, when you can't pull out…"

"You want my knot," I said. "We could be here until the sun rises."

He grinned, nodding as he stroked me with fingers slicked by the most recent dribbles of seed to have escaped me. "I can't think of anything nicer than that. I want you, Reece. I want this, inside me again. You… you want me too, don't you?"

"As if you were my air, my blood," I gasped as his fingers grasped and slipped over the head of my cock. He took what he found there and raised himself up a bit on his knees. He arched his back and used his other hand to pry aside one cheek, and bit his lip as he worked. A moment later he sank back down and angled my cock toward his opening.

The tight ring squeezed against me, but relaxed by degrees as it yielded more to Matthew than to me. Slick with my seed and his spit, my cock speared him slowly, and his ring closed around me. The heat of him, warmed by our unborn child, by that tiny spark of fire that grew in his belly, enveloped me with deliberate leisure, and Matthew's hands dug into my chest as he rode me down. I stared openly at the angelic look of his face, the slight pinch of anticipation at his brow, the part of his lips, and the way his tongue darted across his upper lip as ecstasy seemed to make him glow from within.

Before he even took all of me, the silken tightness of his body had urged my knot halfway out. Almost too much to pass through that gate of pleasure, and I raised my hips as I pushed his down before it swelled to its fullest.

Matthew gave a high-pitched, keening sort of mewl, and if he'd had claws like mine he would have cut me to the ribs. As it was, his fingers dug deep into my flesh. Pain in this body was barely noticeable, but the sting of it heightened the moment as my half-swollen knot passed through that tight barrier. The squeeze of it was enough that in only another few seconds I was full inside him.

"Fuck," he breathed. "Reece, yes… just… just stay like that. Don't move…"

He was not still, though. Matthew's hips twisted as he massaged my knot against the little gland inside him. Each time he did, he gave gasps and coos of pleasure, and my eyes rolled as each squeeze tugged me along closer to a new climax.

I spit on my hand, and reached around his arms to find his cock. The slick stuff spread easily, and he was already leaking freely onto my stomach. Between the two fluids, he glided between my fingers. He tensed as I twisted my palm around the thick meat at the top, and released one hand from my chest to clutch at my wrist. "No, no… not yet, don't make me… please, let me just enjoy it for a moment."

That he was so close, that already his body was reaching its limits just from having me tied to him seemed to make my cock and that knot that was trapped in his body all the more sensitive. I groaned frustration and impatience as I slid my hand down to the base of him and held on to it, anxious to feel the movement of his body as he came for me. I was his, and like this at his mercy—but I wanted him to be mine, as well, subject to my own whims. The instinct to claim burned in my chest, under his touch, and down through my body. I could taste the sweetness of his flesh on my tongue, imagine the sweet smell of his skin as I marked him for all time, for all to see.

It was not a thing to be done without permission. And at the moment, I could not speak. All of me was rapt by the inescapable rocking of his hips, by the insistent tugging at my knot, and by the litany of prayers and curses dripping from his open lips, bridged by moans that were some enchanting music. When he squeezed me just so, and my body reacted with a jerky thrust, he gasped and smiled, and gave the faintest, breathy chuckle. Before long, all those sounds became only one long, low note, and then even that faltered into a ragged, desperate, almost fearful sort of sound.

His shoulders hunched forward. He rocked more urgently, faster, but when I began to stroke him, he clamped his hand down around my wrist. "No, almost… Reece, I'm gonna… you feel so… my fucking god, Reece, make me…"

The rest was only a high-pitched plea as the silken tunnel turned white hot around my cock, and the little gland swelled until I could feel it against my knot. His body thrashed once, and his cock spat a thread of spider silk onto my chest. Then another, stronger, splashed over my neck. A third struck my chin, and I craned my head as I worked against his fading strength to stroke him with a tight fist. His back arched, and another gush burst from him to fall across my lower lip.

Tasting him like that, and the bucking of his hips, and the sound of his release, all worked their magic on me with relentless efficacy, and in another moment I was surging forward, sitting up to wrap my arms around his waist and press my lips to his chest. I found his nipple and sucked hard as fire sparked along the length of my cock and with a cry into his flesh, I convulsed and flooded him with a torrent of my essence. My knot flared the rest of the way, now too thick to possible remove by force. We were tied again, this time intentionally.

As the aftershocks passed through me and out, I drew my legs in to make a proper seat for him, crossing my shins under his buttocks. To accommodate, Matthew worked his legs out from under him and wrapped them around my waist. We adjusted until we were comfortable, with his cheek against mine, my cock buried inside him and twitching, my arms encircling him to hold him close. I breathed in the scents of sweat and life and passion while we caught our breath together, trembling after the ordeal.

"It's incredible," Matthew said softly at my ear. "It feels... I don't even know how to describe it. Perfect. Like two puzzle pieces fitted together that can't be taken apart again."

He nipped at my earlobe and giggled quietly a second before he clenched tight around my knot. As before, the steady trickle of orgasm spiked, and I emptied another pulse of seed into him as I shuddered and squeezed my arms around him tighter.

"I love that," he murmured. "I think... Reece, I think that I love *you*. Is that strange? It's only been two weeks. And it was a fucked-up way to meet. Maybe it's just hormones. Is that a thing with dragon pregnancies? I don't know. It's okay if you... I mean you don't have to say it back. It's just what I'm feeling right now. Is that okay?"

I nuzzled against his neck, kissing him there, and his jaw, and when he finally pulled back just enough, on his lips. It wouldn't do to lie to him. Until and unless I claimed him... "There are things my mind isn't capable of. Not until certain conditions are met. But I have a great fondness for you, and I have not exaggerated what feelings I do have. All of me is yours, Matthew Stiles. Mind, body, and soul. Is that enough for now?"

He kissed me back, and pressed his forehead to mine, smiling. "Yeah, Reece. That's enough for now. Silly dragon."

With that, he squeezed me again, and I keened against his lips as the pressure milked more of me into him.

"You," I gasped, "are relentlessly cruel to me in my most vulnerable moments."

"Better get used to it," Matthew said. "'Cause I'm starting to think everything I ever heard about pregnancy making you horny as hell is one hundred percent true."

Chapter 19
Matthew

While I wouldn't describe what we did as sleeping, I did manage to get some rest, laying my head against Reece's muscular shoulder while he held me through the night. By the time his knot relaxed, and we were able to separate, the sun was just beginning to light the sky. After I made him turn around and let me get rid of some of the mess, we made the awkward walk back to the camp where I could wash properly. That, I decided, was going to be the sort of thing that required more proper planning. I supposed things like airplane sex were out of the question.

Which, I thought as I glanced over at my *mate*, was an odd thought to have. Obviously, we were having a child together. Setting aside the ridiculousness of that situation, which was going to require its own set of navigational coordinates very soon, it did mean that we were going to be connected for a long time. The rest of our lives? I didn't know. Once the baby was here, maybe dragon daddy would steal away to some cave, or tower or… wherever dragons traditionally abided. Or would we buy a house somewhere and settle down? What did it mean to raise a dragon child?

Would they come out as a dragon? If so, birth at a hospital was out of the question. Come to think of it, something told me I did not want to be recorded having a live birth at a hospital at all. That thought triggered a host of other fresh new fears and questions. Where exactly did the baby come out? Because there seemed to be three options. Two of them would probably kill me, and the third didn't seem especially enticing either. How did women *do* this?

By the time we made it to our camper, despite the early hour, there was more than enough activity for us to draw a few pointed, knowing, and even amused looks from diggers making their way to mess for breakfast. Every hour of daylight was valuable, after all. I tried to ignore them, and was thankful that Reece had chosen to shift briefly into and out of a much smaller dragon form—a sight I knew would never cease to floor me with its implications—in order to manifest clothes. These, at my insistence, were somewhat more casual; a pair of plain black pants and a white tee-shirt that hugged his form perfectly. Not that I'd recommended the outfit for that reason alone. It was also more practical in this heat.

Still, it did make him even more easy on the eyes, if that was possible. I let him go ahead of me into the camper, just to get a full view of what was objectively the finest ass in the world, and to see the muscles of his back bunch and stretch as he ascended the stairs.

Once we were inside, I stripped, stuffed my clothes into a hamper, and occupied myself with a short, lukewarm shower that did only what it needed for me and nothing more. I emerged from the cramped little bathroom to find Reece reclined on the bed, staring into some middle distance beyond the ceiling, pensive.

"Everything okay?" I asked as I plucked clean clothes from my suitcase at the other end of the room.

Reece cocked his head at me and said nothing as I dressed, staring quietly.

I tugged my underwear on and frowned at him. "What?"

"Nothing pressing," he said. "I merely enjoy observing you in this state. The shape of your form is pleasing, and now begins to recall fond memories."

I rolled my eyes, but smiled and went just a little pink in the cheeks. "Strange way to say you're checking me out, but I'll take it. I guess you wouldn't be you if you just said things in plain language."

"With practice," Reece said, "I could adapt your vernacular, if you wished it. I have eight centuries of habit to alter, but it would not be the first time. You would hardly recognize the speech of my childhood. Much of it I learned in the thirteenth century of the common era in old Britain, from among the nobility of the day."

I shook my head in amazement as I buttoned my shirt. "You must have seen so much."

Reece nodded. "More than a human generally does. But in blocks of time, not continuously. During periods of growth, it is necessary to retreat into the wild places, to hunt regularly, and to shed old scales."

Yet another question occurred to me, one with a sobering weight to it. "So, our child then," I said. "How long does this last? Pregnancy, I mean. Uh, how long until he or she is born?"

"Twelve months," Reece said.

"And after that?" I wondered.

He shrugged. "I understand that humans raise their young, do they not?"

"Well, of course *we* do, I'm asking if you do." I stepped into a pair of sturdy cargo shorts. "That is, if you do it with us. Will I be there? Or do you, you know... I mean there's not exactly a kindergarten program for little dragons, you know? How will we live once the baby is here? I'm not exactly excited at the prospect of living out in the wild."

Reece smiled, and shook his head. "That will not be necessary. Until the child is in his twenties—it is unlikely our pairing will produce a female—he will not have the requisite strength of spirit to change his form. At that time, I will take him into a remote place, and instruct him in the way of it. Until that time... I suppose I will live with the both of you as a man."

Great sex—especially the kind that last for hours and you can literally pass out while still having it because you can't actually stop it happening—has a way of sneaking into a person's brain and shutting down some really important faculties like reason and long-term thinking. Reece, however, had just told me that we were committed for the next twenty years or so. My longest relationship had only lasted four years. And they'd started out not entirely different than this one.

I wasn't sure what to ask or say next, so I focused on putting my socks and shoes on instead, and then with making my hair look something roughly in sight of presentable. In the end, I just put a cap on. In a few hours it would be matted and sweaty anyway.

Reece watched me all the while, and each time I glanced at him to see those calm eyes and that nearly blank expression he looked just a little more... saurian, each time. Emotions were a monkey-brain thing, neurologically. Did he even feel things the way I did? It certainly sounded like it. Maybe he didn't use the word love—and maybe I had used it a bit too quickly and under neurological duress—but he did say that he belonged to me entirely. Was that kind of love?

I wished I knew if it was a language barrier or something deeper than that. "I guess we should rejoin the world," I said. "Um... so when it's time for the baby to come. We can't go to a hospital because male pregnancy would raise a few questions that would never go away. Especially if the answer was 'dragon magic'. This order of midwives is apparently defunct. So I have to ask... what do we do?"

Now, that passive expression showed a hint of worry. One that Reece was good at covering quickly, but only after I'd gotten a look at it. "We will consult with some who might know more."

"Is there like... some kind of paternal mortality rate I should know about?" I was drumming my fingers on the counter without realizing it, and stopped to stuff my hands in my pockets.

Reece leaned forward to rest his elbows on his knees, his hands clasped. "You are worried for your survival."

"Was it the word 'mortality' that gave it away, or the look of abject terror on my face?"

He stood and came to me, and took my hands in his. "Matthew," he said with that spine-melting gentleness he had shown me often the past couple of weeks, "I do not have all, or even very many, of the answers. It is new to me as well. But there are others for whom these things are well known."

"But we can't ask them because I'm sort of committing some statutory rape for dragons," I said. "Isn't that the case? Who can we ask?"

"There are those among my people who are... outside of the common society. Some of them are old and wise." He dropped his eyes. "If need be, I will approach them. Tradition, law, society—these things are the roots of my people. But for our child, and for you, I would turn from them to seek the answers we require."

"I know," I said, and squeezed his hands. "Hey. Reece, in all of this, you're the one that I trust. I'm just scared. It's not normal for humans. You'll just have to indulge me a little bit, okay?"

He met my eyes again, and I kissed him to reassure him that I wasn't angry, or blaming him. "Come on. There's work to do, if we're going to stay here a while. And the more familiar with those remains we are, the better the chances I can figure out how to convince Taylor he's wrong about them."

Which was its own special kind of unsolvable riddle. But—one thing at a time, right? We left the camper, and focused on our next immediate task, which was breakfast.

Because 'eating for two'? It's absolutely a thing.

Chapter 20
Reece

The longer a dragon spends in human shape, the more human-like we gradually become. Between our coupling in the desert and Matthew's admission of his many fears, I determined that it would be best to eschew my dragon body for a time. There were things, I sensed, that he desired of me that I was not easily able to give him as I was. Like Tarin, I needed to immerse myself in being human to an extent that was somewhat unnerving, if I am to tell the truth of the matter.

For the three weeks that followed the revelation, I did not shift at all. I worked in the dig, alongside Joseph at times—who had the acuity of sense not to pry regarding Matthew's slip of the tongue—and at others, when I was able, alongside Matthew. When Matthew was not nearby, I did my best to keep tabs on him without employing my dragon's senses. Even changing my eyes or ears made it difficult to maintain a human perspective consistently.

Matthew, for his part, showed himself to be a gentle, affectionate, and attentive mate. His hunger for me seemed insatiable, more than a match for my own, and on several occasions he woke in the night and, without warning, aroused me and took sustenance from my seed. When I used this word, however, he made a face that suggested it was not the correct concept in operation.

"It's not... I don't do it for nutrition, Reece," he said, his chest and shoulder trembling with quiet laughter barely contained. "I just like doing it. And I like that you like it. It's just for feeling good, that's all. Sustenance... *Jesus wept*. Just say swallowed, or sucked you off, or something normal. Anything that doesn't sound like I woke up hungry. Please."

It took effort, concentrated and persistent, to gradually learn some of his vernacular. Often, I misused his idioms and he gently corrected me. Were I much younger, and still immature, I might have taken offense, but the sound of his laughter—full or subtle—engendered a kind of sweetness of the mind; I enjoyed it, and sometimes made mistakes on purpose just to see that struggle take place on his lips and in his eyes.

The times that were the sweetest, though, were the quiet, private moments between sunset and sunrise—those moments when we lay beside one another, and I rested my hand on his belly and tried to feel the growth of life within him. Moments when Matthew would gaze into my eyes, a smile playing over his lips that was not humorous, but rather endeared. As if he felt something that simply gave him wordless joy.

The longer I spent in a human body, the easier it was to feel the first inklings of that joy myself. Me, and my mate, and our child.

A family.

Matthew had been ensconced in Professor Taylor's tent for hours. Mercy had taken lunch to them both, though I offered to do so myself. I was told that they were quite busy, and suppressed a desire to explain where in the hierarchy of nature she and Taylor existed, relative to a dragon and his mate. But, while it was known by now that Matthew and I were 'involved' as many used the word, this separation was not seen as problematic by any but myself.

"He'll be safe here," Joseph insisted as we left the mess tent after lunch and returned to the dig. Much of the dragon—a female, as Joseph had speculated before—was now uncovered, and there was new work of ensuring that each part was kept whole and safe as the rest of the dig continued to unearth the portions still in the earth but obscured by the rest of the remains. It was slow and complicated work.

"His safety is a concern," I admitted, "but it is more than that. I do not like to be far from him. The feeling is uncomfortable. As if everything is slightly more difficult when he is not near me."

"What," Joseph asked, grinning, "you mean hard to breathe? Hard to eat? Hard to sleep or think?"

"I will not require sleep for some time yet," I corrected him, "but the rest... that is an apt description."

Joseph looked to the sky as if seeking aid or advice. "You people. No offense. Have you considered that maybe you're in love with him?"

"Matthew and I have discussed this previously," I said as we descended into the pit via the steps, and picked our way carefully among the strings and posts that formed the 'grid'. "He has confessed his love to me. I have stated my unwavering dedication to his well-being."

The Wolven grunted and looked me over, whistling. "Wow. He must *really* love you to put up with that."

We took up small buckets and collected tools, and moved to the nearly unearthed skull, where we had been carefully removing soil that morning. There was something soothing about the work. It was precise, and time-consuming, and required a great deal of concentration. I welcomed the distraction. Especially given the current circumstances. "In his condition," I said softly, "it may well be difficult to properly assess what he is feeling. It is difficult for me as well. There are factors involved that are not common to human experience."

Joseph groaned. "Your kind is always overanalyzing everything. Swear, you think with your lizard brain. You think my people aren't familiar with the influence of nature? We mate for life too, you know. You're not that special."

"Perhaps you do," I said as I began brushing away the soil immediately below the hollow where the dragon's tympanic structure would have been in life, "but humans do not. It would be wise for the two of us to curtail such talk until after... that is, until the current situation has reached its conclusion."

Again, Joseph whistled his amazement, though I understood instinctively that it was not praise. "Claiming for you all must be very different than it is for us."

It was not his concern, but the jab rankled. "I have not... claimed him as such. Yet."

The Wolven paused, and peered at me in confusion. "You put a baby in there and didn't claim him? That's cold, cousin."

"You wouldn't understand," I growled. "The situation is more complex than one of your kind would understand. Our culture has a deeper respect for tradition and law, it is the cornerstone of our—"

"Oh, fuck you," Joseph muttered. "You all think you're the only people that understand those things, so high and mighty just because you've been around for longer than everyone else. Let me tell you something, to my people it would be shameful not to claim your mate. A slap in the face that would be unforgivable. You want to know tradition and law? To us, that's a one-way ticket to a grave. Maybe we're a little more compassionate about some things, but nothing is more important than that bond. Not even law."

"There are complicating factors," I said. Some of the workers appeared to be interested in our conversation, I realized. I cleared my throat. "Which you would not comprehend. I appreciate your concern, however inappropriate, on the status of a relationship which has naught to do with you, but I can assure you that it is well in hand."

"Is that what he thinks?" he asked.

I started to answer him, but realized that I did not know for certain, and did not wish to speak falsely on a subject I was not confident to accurately portray. Matthew didn't know about the claiming, or what it would mean—or why I resisted it.

"If he is unhappy—"

Joseph straightened, and held a hand up. "You hear that?"

I didn't at first; not with my human ears. After a few moments, however, the faint sound of an engine was audible, and then tires churning the parched ground. "Someone's coming."

The Wolven nodded, and did not look as though he had expected an arrival. "Could be people coming to pick up samples."

"Could be Templars," I muttered.

We put our tools down and hurried up the steps. We nearly slammed into two workers bringing back empty buckets, and muttered apologies as they slipped past us before we stood in the opening to the tent.

Outside, a boxy but remarkably reflective Humvee parked near the middle of the camp. The engine cut off, and a tall, balding man who held himself like a person familiar with violence emerged from the driver's side and circled around to open the passenger side rear door. From there, a thick-bodied man with a cane—but no apparent difficulty walking—emerged and glanced around the camp with open disdain before brushing off his black jacket.

At a glance? Perhaps it was paranoia—but they dressed like the men who'd attacked Matthew. Templars.

It was only an instinct, but it was powerful. "Joseph," I murmured, "do you have people nearby?"

"Closest is two or three hours," he said. "Why? Those look like the money guys. Rich, you know? Why else would they be here?"

"They may be more than merely that, if indeed that is their nature," I said. "It is possible they are Templars. I need to locate and secure Matthew."

"Oh, he left about ten minutes ago."

I frowned at Joseph. "What? Why? How do you know?"

He thumbed his left ear. "I heard him and Mercy talking about taking a walk. You're really committing to this no-shifting thing, huh?"

"Less committed by the second now," I said. "I must observe these men, see who they are and what they're doing here. They could be looking for my mate. I must beg a favor."

"Go look after your mate?" Joseph guessed.

I nodded. "At a distance. It would be a great comfort to me. And I will repay the favor when you have need."

"Favor from a dragon," Joseph murmured. "Yeah, okay. I'll take it."

He alerted the other workers that he had something to take care of, and slipped out of the back side of the tent. As much as I wished to meet Matthew on his native ground, I shifted my inner ear as I strode out of the tent with an empty bucket from the entrance, and angled my hearing toward Professor Taylor's tent.

"…to see the specimen for myself," a man's smooth, deep voice was saying. "The findings you've submitted so far are very promising. Just the sort of thing I and my associates were hoping you would uncover."

"I'm pleased to know I've lived up to your expectations," Taylor replied. "The work itself is immeasurably rewarding. A dragon—you must understand, this is the culmination of my life's—"

"As much as it pleases me to know how enthused you are, Professor," the man with the deep voice said, "I'd just as soon skip the inspirational talk and go right to the main event? Show me the specimen. I've paid a lot of money for this little sightseeing trip."

"Oh," Taylor said, thoroughly cowed. "Yes, of course. Right this way, I'll show you myself. It's quite—"

"Just lead the way, Professor. Less talking."

I stepped behind one of the campers as feet shuffled, and watched as they emerged and made their way around the edge of the dig tent to the opened flap. Once they were inside, the man with the deep voice spoke again, and it was all I needed to hear to know for certain what he was.

"At last," he said, with the reverence of the fanatical, "there you are. We can finally end this."

Chapter 21
Matthew

Mercy and I strolled through the brush some distance from the dig. It was still visible behind us, but although Reece was on this 'staying human' kick, I didn't know how committed he was to it. He had great ears, and I needed privacy.

"It's so easy to forget how beautiful the land is here," Mercy said as she paused to stretch her hands over her head. She spread her arms wide afterward, and seemed to soak up the sun. "Out here in the real world, where it's still pure. This was a good idea."

"Yeah," I said as I scuffed a rust-colored rock out of the ground with my toe. "It's great. Um... so, you know, I find myself wondering... you're a doula, right? Among other things. I'm not actually sure I know what that is. Is it like a... midwife?"

Mercy dropped her arms and gave me a patient look. "Not exactly. A doula is like a coach. A midwife delivers babies. Or they can. I've done a lot of home births. Think of me as like... a new mom's best friend for hire. Not that I do it just for the money. Well, *did* it for the money—I haven't acted as a doula in a few years. But it's all about being present, and focused on the mom, and reminding her to breathe, and be encouraging and... lots of stuff. Why do you ask?"

I pursed my lips. That didn't sound remotely like what I needed. I was nervous enough having this conversation at all. Mercy seemed earnest, and made a big deal about 'honoring space' and 'sacred trust' and things like that. What I wanted was to talk to Yuri but I didn't want to put him in any danger. Mercy was the next best thing—and just, ah, *eccentric* enough to be open-minded about things. Plus, she'd identified my pregnancy first, and still seemed to give me the side-eye once in a while. I didn't think I was showing, but... had I put on just a little paunch in the last couple of weeks? I wished I had a scale.

"Just curious," I said. "But let's say, in the midst of an emergency. Like a woman on her way to the hospital in a cab, but the traffic is bad and she'll never make it in time. Could you... you know, like, deliver a baby?"

Mercy knelt by a bush and poked her finger into it. When she stood, she was grinning at a ladybug. "Good luck in some cultures, you know?" She sighed, and let it go back to its home when it fluttered off the tip of her finger. "I guess I've seen enough births that I could muddle through it. Assuming there were no complications."

"Complications," I echoed. "Like what?"

She shrugged. "Gosh, all sorts of things. Childbirth is, like, *really* dangerous. You wouldn't believe all the ways it can get you. You can bleed out, rupture an organ, have a stroke, an aneurysm, even—"

"I think I get the picture," I said quickly. Was I sweating? I decided it was the heat, though lately the heat didn't bother me quite as much as it used to. I dropped my hand from my stomach and occupied it with my pocket. When that seemed awkward, I kicked at the rock again and then bent to pick it up. "Hey what kind of rock is this?"

Mercy leaned in, critical. "That... is a chunk of dense, dry soil." She took it from my open hand and gave it a squeeze. It crumbled to dust. "See? Matt, I'm happy you wanted to go on a walk, I think you're fascinating and you have one of the most interesting auras I've encountered. Well, second most. Oh, okay, it's tied. Maybe I should get you two in touch with one another, that would be—sorry; never mind. I'm just wondering if there's a reason you seem a little nervous and frazzled."

"I have something I need to tell you," I blurted. "Or... I guess I just really *want* to tell you. Or someone, anyone—no offense—but since you're, well, *you*, I think maybe you're the best option. And it's a long way off but you're the closest thing I have to a midwife, so—"

Mercy's jaw dropped. "Oh. My. Goddess. You *are* pregnant. I knew it! The unakite never lies. Wow. This is just... wow. Wow."

This was probably how a cell in a petri dish felt. Mercy circled me, looking me over like she could somehow see whatever it was that made me different if she looked hard enough. "Yep. I'm pregnant."

"How?" she asked. "Never mind. How? I mean, who's the father? Well, obviously you are. Or, oh! Is there a mother? Like a reverse impregnation or—duh, never mind. Of course, it must be Reece."

I groaned, and turned so we were facing one another again. "Does everyone know?"

"Oh." She laughed and nodded enthusiastically. "Oh, yeah. Everyone knows. They all figure it's none of their business but that man watches you like you're going to fall over any—ah. That makes sense now. How sweet! But how did it happen? Oh my goddess, is he an alien? Were you abducted? Or did you fall in love? That is so cute. You get abducted, they implant a fetus, but then he falls in love and rescues you and brings you to the middle of nowhere to avoid recapture by the mothership? Is that what happened? Because that would be such a sweet—"

"Mercy," I hissed. When she recoiled, I closed my eyes and calmed myself. I put my hands up for peace. "I'm sorry. It's not any of that. Reece isn't an alien. Not... exactly."

"So then what is he?" she asked. Her eyes widened, and she pointed at me. "Or what are you? Are you the alien?"

"Mercy, no one is an alien." I ran my fingers through my hair. "Look... you can't tell anyone about this. Not Taylor, not any of the workers, not your closest friends or family. It's a huge secret, and you have to know that if anyone found out, I'd be locked up and observed and maybe even cut into pieces. This is life and death serious, okay?"

She nodded, still wide-eyed and eager. When I didn't immediately tell her what that secret was, she crossed her heart twice. When I still didn't get the words out, she pushed harder. "I swear on my crystal collection. No! On my karma. Telling secrets is very bad for your energy."

"Well, that's comforting," I muttered.

"Oh, but not for you. I mean... other people's secrets."

I didn't believe in dragons, magic rocks, men getting pregnant, or Templars until recently, so the karma comment did give me pause. But it seemed like sound logic and besides—I didn't know how long we would be here and it wasn't like I wanted to look up just any midwife. Reece said he *might* be able to find information, but what if he couldn't? I needed someone crazy enough to be in my pocket, on my side. Just in case. It felt like the kind of secret that could cause as much problem for her as it would for me.

"If I tell you this," I said, unwilling to throw her any further into the deep end, "I think... Mercy, it might make things sort of dangerous for you. Some people came after me, before."

Mercy sobered some. She looked up at the sky, obviously giving it real thought. Or asking the universe for guidance that, for all I knew, it gave her. She looked back to me and gave a solemn sort of nod. "Matt, if you want me to know, then I want to know. Even if it is dangerous. I'm an explorer and a scientist—I can't just turn away from something like this. And it sounds like you need as many friends as you can get."

I breathed a sigh of mixed relief and guilt before the words tumbled out of me. Until I started speaking, I didn't even realize just how much I needed to say them.

"Reece is the father," I admitted. "He's a dragon, Mercy. And they don't have females so instead they have to breed with, um…. Well he says 'sacred' omega but I don't think I'm particularly sacred I think it's just like a thing they say. But that's me. I'm that, and now I'm pregnant, and I'm scared out of my mind and have no idea who to turn to because this apparently hasn't happened for a long time and no one really knows how it's going to go so you're pretty much all I've got right now and I need someone to help me get through this because I'm this close to breaking down from one hour to the next and keeping it together is making me crazy."

Mercy's eyes had grown progressively larger, her jaw dropping lower as I blustered through everything in my brain. When I was done, I waited for her to run and tell Taylor, proving that I'd made a horrible misjudgment about the kind of person she was.

Instead, she put her arms out and pulled me into a tight, warm, wordless hug. At first I thought it lasted far too long. After several seconds, though, it was like she'd squeezed something inside me tight enough that it cracked. I put my arms around her in return, and my eyes burned as I struggled to hold back a sob.

"It's okay to be afraid," she said. "And it's okay to show it, Matt. No matter how it happens, pregnancy and childbirth are scary. Exciting, hopefully, and full of joy—but it's an ordeal no matter how you feel about it and believe me, it's okay to not be okay even if you're happy. Let it out; I'm here for you."

I did let it out. I sobbed against her shoulder, and it was the strangest mix of emotion I'd ever experienced. I was scared, and excited, and relieved that someone else knew. She let me go on without comment, either encouragement or judgment, until finally the crying session ended gradually on its own.

When that last sob was out of me, and I'd wiped my nose and eyes on my shirt for lack of anything else to do it with, Mercy finally spoke. "If you want me to help," she said, "then I will help. It would be best if I could talk to Reece, or anyone familiar with how this all works. But we can just wing it if we need to. So… is that why you're here? Because of the dragon remains? I mean, is that why Reece is here?"

I shook my head. "No. Neither of us knew. There are some people who kind of make it their business to get rid of dragons. Templars, like the old order of the Templars. Same people, I guess. And part of their mission is to get rid of me."

Mercy's jaw clacked shut, and she bit her lower lip as she folded her arms. "Oh, dear. Well… that's not good."

"No, it really isn't," I sighed.

But Mercy shook her head slowly and glanced back at the dig. "That's not what I mean. It's super-secret, and Doc and I signed a lot of papers to keep it that way, but that was before all this. Matt, the people that hold the company we're being financed through… they're called Templar Industries. And now, I can't imagine that's a coincidence."

"Shit," I breathed.

"Shit is right," someone said.

Mercy and I both startled as we swiveled around to the source of the voice.

It was Joseph. He hadn't made a sound as he approached. How much had he heard?

"J-Joseph," I stammered. "What are you… what's going on? Why are you out here?"

"Reece sent me," he said, hands spread. "It's okay. I know all about what's going on. And I guess Mercy does, too, now. Don't know if that was smart or not but, in any case, you can't go back to the camp just yet."

"Why?" Mercy and I asked at the same time.

Joseph glanced back that direction, craning his neck as if trying to see something. "Because if those are the people bankrolling this project, we're pretty sure someone from Templar Industries just showed up."

Chapter 22
Reece

The conversation between Taylor and the man with the cane did not go well inside the dig tent, or back at Taylor's tent afterward. Mr. de Payens, as Taylor named him, wanted the remains packed up within the next month and shipped to his facility in Dallas. Taylor contested that rushing the dig for a specific deadline could endanger the integrity of the remains.

"I'm not remotely interested in the integrity of the bones," de Payens informed Taylor.

Taylor sputtered. "But… there's so much to learn from them, and if they're ever to be put on display—"

"Professor Taylor," de Payens interrupted, "tell me where in the project briefing is there any mention of displaying the bones anywhere."

Taylor paused. "Well, I—I just assumed, given the magnitude of this discovery…"

"That's where you went wrong," de Payens said. "You made an assumption. You're being paid for your expertise, and your silence, Professor. But you were chosen because you've got no academic standing. Once this is all over, you'll get your final check, and our thanks, and you'll go on your way and keep this to yourself. And should you speak a word of it, the NDAs you signed are extensive and cover a broad range of possibilities, from sworn statements all the way to parody use. My people will make sure that you are broke, unemployable, and the laughingstock of the academic world. Have I made myself sufficiently clear?"

The professor's voice was shaky when he answered, something just above a croak. "You have, Mr. de Payens. Perfectly."

It seemed like they would leave then. I had a choice to make. If I intervened now, I could make an introduction, perhaps learn something more. Or I could stay out of sight, and question Taylor afterward. Drawing attention to myself could put me square in the cross-hairs of de Payens and his people, if they didn't already know who I was. If they did, I could expect them to move quickly.

Of course, there was a third option as well. Follow them into the desert in my dragon form, under cover of a concealment spell, and melt their vehicle to slag with them inside it. That, though, would draw even more attention—and Templars would not wonder what caused such a fire.

In the end I decided to keep my distance. It was more important to know what de Payens believed he had found in the skeleton, and to ensure Matthew's continued safety, than to spark a confrontation. And if he believed anything to be amiss, he might accelerate his timeline. As it was, a month was not long to do what was required here.

De Payens and his man stalked out of Taylor's tent, and I busied myself with pretending to dump dirt out of my bucket and onto the pile before I turned and made my way back to the dig site, careful not to show any particular interest in the visitors. I did hear Taylor, however, making something of a mess in his tent.

When they finally pulled away, I put the bucket down in the dig tent and resisted the urge to go and find Joseph and Matthew. I trusted Joseph to have an ear pointed toward camp, and to see to Matthew's safety for the moment. Instead, I made my way to Taylor's tent and pushed the flap aside to peer in.

There were papers strewn over the ground, and some of Taylor's instruments had been swept onto the rugs as well. He had his face in his hands and was muttering to himself. "Should have known those corporate bastards wouldn't be interested in scientific achievement. Well, they can all eat shit. I'm already as fucked as I can possibly get. Zelniky—he'll back me up if he sees what I've found here, I should—"

"Professor?" I inquired as I stepped through the flap.

Taylor straightened and thrust his hands into his pockets. His eyes were puffy, but if they'd been wet before he had dried them now. "M-Mr. Smith," he stammered, and took in the mess he'd made furtively. "I... fell. Barely caught myself. Seem to have made a mess. How can I help you?"

This was a man who clearly desired recognition for discovering proof of my people. I had to be careful how I approached the subject. Taylor could in no way be trusted to keep a secret. "I happened to overhear some of what your patron said. I understand this project isn't to be made public?"

He cleared his throat and waved a hand. "We're in negotiation. I assure you, you'll be credited—"

"That is not my concern, Professor," I said as I knelt to scoop up some of the papers. When I did, Taylor joined me as well, righting a waste basket and picking up the instruments he'd swept off his desk.

"What is your concern then, Mr. Smith?" He asked, adjusting his microscope to fit neatly into its previous place. He seemed to occupy himself with it for an unnecessarily long time.

I placed the papers on the larger table, frowning. "My concern is the nature of the company that you've allied yourself with for this endeavor."

He continued to fidget with the microscope. "There's no reason to be concerned. I assure you, they are a reputable organization."

"I believe it is possible they are in fact quite dangerous."

Taylor froze, and then turned slowly to face me. "What do you know about de Payens?"

"Nothing," I admitted. "His visit to the project was my first observation of him. However, I have known many men like him. I believe if you elected to expose this project to others, he would do more than ruin your reputation and financial security."

The professor's eyes narrowed, his lips pinched in a scowl as he jabbed a finger at me. "You didn't overhear anything. You were eavesdropping. I could throw you out of this camp for that. What did you hear?"

"Enough to convince me that I am correct in my assessment of de Payens," I replied. "You cannot expose yourself to his wrath. It would be the end of you. However, neither can you concede to his demand. He must not be allowed to take these remains with him to his facility."

Taylor threw his hands up and laughed bitterly. "How very helpful of you to say so. Here I was trying to figure out what to do, and your very keen suggestion is that I not only keep it to myself and consider the last three months wasted, but I also snub the man you think might kill me if I don't do as he says. So it's a choice between obscurity and poverty, or death, is it? I'm a scientist, Mr. Smith. Progress and knowledge are all that matter to me. I'll thank you to see yourself out, and leave me to make my own decisions informed by my own ideals."

There was of course the unspoken option, which I hoped to avoid. If my people should be alerted, that would put an end to all of this quickly, and brutally. I could not warn him of that, of course. And there were other consequences to consider. None of these were decisions I felt I should make on my own, without consulting Matthew. "I will leave you then."

He only flailed a hand as he turned away, shooing me out of his tent. When I left, I caught movement in the corner of my eye, and looked out into the desert to see Matthew returning in the company of Joseph and Mercy. There was an unfamiliar look on Mercy's face. Something like awe, perhaps. It made the pit of my stomach twist. *Matthew, tell me you didn't.*

I walked out to meet them halfway. "Thank you, Joseph," I said as I reached them, nodding my thanks to the Wolven before I settled my gaze on Matthew. "How was your... outing?"

Matthew's cheeks flushed redder than the sun alone had made them. His eyes darted to Mercy and back, and then sought the ground rather than my no doubt darkening countenance. "Mercy knows, Reece. I'm sorry. I just had to talk to someone, and I need help with this that you've already said you can't give me with any certainty."

"Knows what exactly?" I asked, turning the same look on the young woman.

Mercy *curtsied*. As if I were a lord. "I swear, your secret is safe with me, Mister... er, do I call you something special? Lord Dragon, or—"

"You can call me Reece, Mercy, which is my name," I said through my teeth. "And whatever it is that you *think* you know, be advised that it is knowledge which could cause a great deal of harm—to myself, but also to Matthew, to you, and to your Professor Taylor. And to many others besides, were it wielded irresponsibly. Not limited to everyone in this camp."

I had not seen fear on Mercy's face before—she was, I thought, so proactively positive that it was simply an emotion she did not have within her. Clearly, I was wrong about that. She paled, and swallowed loudly, and her head vibrated as she nodded quickly. "I won't talk," she squeaked. "Promise."

I heaved a great sigh, and pulled Matthew to me to wrap my arms around him. He'd been crying, I thought, but I did not wish to bring this to the attention of either Mercy or Joseph. A tight muscle somewhere in my thoughts unwound slowly as I absorbed the comfort of having him in sight and under my protection again. "I prefer that you inform me when you intend to leave my vicinity. I cannot protect you if I do not know where you are."

"That was the point," Matthew replied, his face buried in my chest. "I needed this, Reece. I'm sorry I didn't ask you first, but I don't have anyone here."

"You have me," I told him.

He tilted his head up. "You know what I mean."

Perhaps I did. Still, I gave Mercy a hard eye to reinforce my early mandate.

She clasped her hands over her chest as if in prayer, and smiled nervously at me. "I have so many questions."

Chapter 23
Matthew

The four of us convened in Mercy's tent. The camper was too small for us to all fit in comfortably, and while Mercy's tent was close to Taylor's, Joseph assured us that no one was listening in on us.

"How's that now?" I asked. I looked back and forth between Joseph and Reece, and pointed at the worker. "Is he a dragon, too?"

"No," Joseph said. "Something different."

"This day gets more interesting by the minute," Mercy murmured.

"For now, it's enough to know that Joseph has keen senses," Reece said. "He is a true ally, though, and will not betray us."

I gave up on trying to get more answers. These people and their secrets. "Fine. So… this place is run by Templars. Which we were explicitly trying to avoid. Now they want those bones and probably for nothing good. Do they know I'm here? Is that why Professor Taylor invited me?"

Mercy shook her head. "I don't think so… or if it is why, I don't think he knew. Doc can be fanatical, but he's not violent. If he knew it would put you in any danger, he wouldn't have brought you in."

"Still," Reece said, "it is possible this is how the men who came for you previously knew that you were here. They may have intercepted communications from Taylor's end."

"So I left my phone in Catarina for nothing?" I asked.

Reece gave me a long-suffering look. "It was the most correct tactical decision in the moment. I will procure you another phone in the future if the opportunity arises, Matthew."

I rocked back in the chair Mercy had given me, and put my hands up in surrender. "It was just a comment."

"The question is," Joseph spoke up, "if they did know, then don't they know he's arrived?"

"It seems likely," Reece agreed. "But they've made one failed assault already. Perhaps they do not wish to endanger the dig, and cannot be certain of the fate of the first pair. Templars are cautious, careful. Their greatest strength in the old days was their ability to communicate covertly, to observe, and plan. My people believe the sacred omegas to be extinct. They had no reason to believe that one of us would intervene. It was only through luck or fate that I was informed of Matthew's existence to begin with."

Silence fell softly for a moment as four brains made loud thoughts.

"What do they want the bones for?" Mercy asked. "If they're committed to secrecy, then they aren't intending to put them on display, like you heard de Payens saying. So what's the point? Do they collect them?"

Reece shook his head. "I do not know the answer to that, and it concerns me greatly. De Payens seemed excited, and said 'we can finally end this'. What he meant specifically, I cannot say. But the Templars have one primary goal, and that is to put an end to my people entirely. Hunting and dispatching our sacred omegas is no doubt a part of that plan. But what role the bones of a female dragon might play is a mystery to me."

"Is there anyone who might know?" I asked. "Some… dragon scientist or something?"

Reece shook his head slowly. "Not as such. Our people do not rely on technology. We have no need." A crease appeared between his eyebrows, and he frowned thoughtfully. "However, there are those who live among humans by necessity. It is possible there is one among them who might be better equipped."

"Anyone we can contact?" Joseph asked. "You're talking about outcasts, right?"

"Yes," Reece muttered. "And it is possible to contact at least one of them. He may know of others. To do so, though…"

Joseph spread his hands. "You can't go to the elders or the ancients, right?"

Reece shook his head. "Not unless the need becomes dire. And even then I would prefer to avoid them if possible. Still, begging aid from outcasts will create its own problems."

Mercy was practically on the verge of falling off her seat. "Ancients? Elders? Are those generational markers? Your society is tiered by age and experience? And outcasts—what are those, criminals?"

I saw the impatience and irritation in the flexing of Reece's jaw. "Let's just save questions for a better time," I suggested.

"Right," Mercy said, and leaned back in her chair, her foot tapping quickly on the carpet. "Right, of course. Sorry. Carry on."

Reece paced the length of the tent and back, his arms folded over his chest, his head bowed as he thought something over. The conclusion he came to was not apparently a happy one. "I believe Joseph may have identified the most tactical option," he said finally. "The outcasts will not only guard our secret, but have a vested interest in seeing an end to the Templar threat. They do not have the protection of society at large, and are vulnerable. It is possible the ancients would only counsel patience and hiding—that is their way, and it will take them decades to decide anything. The elders will not act without the approval of the ancients. The outcasts may be less bound by our traditions, and subject to disagreement, but at least they will act quickly. Some among them I count as friends of old."

"Great," I said. "So call them up. Do you think some of them might know a bit more about how this whole pregnancy thing plays out?"

"There are not many of them," Reece said. "But perhaps. I will inquire. The problem, however, is that in order to contact them I will have to travel. And I cannot take you with me."

My stomach twisted. "What? Why not? We can take a car, you don't have to fly me into the—"

"If he takes you out of the camp," Joseph said, "and it turns out the Templars are watching you, they'll move as soon as you're in the open, before you can get back to a crowded place."

My mouth dried, and my heart beat a little faster. "But… if I stay, then who's to say they won't move as soon as they know Reece is gone?"

"Because," Mercy said, "they'd have to kill everyone here to cover their tracks. Right? And why do that when they can just wrap up the dig in a month, and make their move then. To get out of here, you've got to cross a lot of mostly unpopulated land and very small towns. But the dig had to be registered with the state. The government knows we're here, and so do the local municipalities. It was a whole thing, we had to get four different permits."

I stood from my chair. "Reece, I don't want to be here without you. If they come for me again—"

"My people will guard the camp," Joseph said. "I can call in a few favors, get four or five to patrol, just out of sight. They've got as much beef with the Templars as Reece's people do. Of course… they'd feel better about protecting a claimed mate…"

Reece and Joseph shared a look that I thought was going to escalate to violence. Reece's nostrils flared, and he stared Joseph down. Or tried to at any rate. Joseph shot back casual defiance, one eyebrow quirked.

"Beg your pardon?" I asked, both to get their attention and to hopefully interrupt whatever was about to happen. "I'm his mate. I've got his kid in my belly for about the next year or so. You can't get more mated than that. Can you?"

Joseph turned to the tent flap. "I'll get in touch with my people. You talk to your mate."

Reece watched him go, and wouldn't look at me when Joseph was gone. "Mercy… may we have the room?"

Mercy read the room—or the energy, maybe, because it was definitely tense enough that even I could feel it—and quickly got to her feet. "Absolutely. Take as long as you need. I'll see what I can find out from Taylor."

She hurried out, and left me and Reece alone. I tried to get him to meet my eyes, but he turned away and paced again. "Okay," I said as I tracked him back and forth, "so I take it there's some new thing I need to know. What did Joseph mean by that? 'Claimed Mate'. Do you need like some kind of deed to me or something? Is this ye olde dragon patriarchy tradition or…?"

"Joseph spoke out of turn," Reece grumbled.

"That sounds a lot like he said something I should know, but that you haven't told me and were hoping he wouldn't mention," I said. I stepped in front of Reece and forced him to look at me. "Reece—what is the big deal?"

He put his hands on my cheeks. "Matthew, it doesn't—"

"Stop." I reached up and put my hands on his. "Reece, you can't keep me in the dark. I'm going to have our *child*. Do you really think I can just live the rest of my life without answers? What will we teach our son? What part do you expect me to play, if I don't know anything about him, or you, or this culture that, like it or not, I'm a part of now. Stop treating me like I can't handle knowing too much. I'm in this, I'm not trying to get out of it. Okay?"

He looked tortured. Like I had stabbed him. His hands fell away, but I held them tight.

Reece nodded at last. "Of course. You have the right to know."

"So?" I pressed. "Tell me."

He took a long breath, and exhaled through tight lips as he sought out a place to sit. I pulled my chair close, and took his hand again to hold onto it while he got whatever it was out. Something about the way he held himself made me think this was going to be difficult.

"When a dragon takes a mate," he said at length, "there is more to it than knotting and progeny. Even without progeny in play, it is customary for us to then claim our mates."

"I'd say I'm pretty damn claimed," I said, trying to lighten the moment. "Sometimes you're all I can think about, and let me tell you I'm falling—"

"It's different," Reece breathed. "Claiming is a spiritual bond. It is a means of binding dragon and mate together, permanently. You could compare it to marriage, but the claiming bond cannot be abandoned through something as trivial as divorce. It is a bond for life, incontrovertible, unbreakable. Only the death of one mate can dissolve it. By tradition, it also means that we would share our fates, should my people elect to punish me for what I have done."

A familiar hurt squeezed at my heart. I held on to Reece's hand, even though there was a moment when I wanted to let it go. "So let me just... what you're saying is that there is something that we could do, that would somehow commit us to one another. But you don't want to do that thing. Even though I'm having your child."

"It is not so simple as that," he said, and turned his hand over under mine so that our palms pressed together. "All that I have to give you, Matthew, the only life I can offer, is tied to the Hoard. The shared wealth of my people. If we were discovered, it is possible they would take you from me, so that you could be cared for—so that our child would be cared for—while I could be made an outcast. If I claimed you, your fate and mine would be inextricably linked. You would be outcast with me, and I could offer you nothing. Our son would be born with nothing, no connection to his people. You cannot want this."

I did let his hand go, so that I could stand and pace, trying to shake a growing sense of déjà vu. "How is it is possible that I could have this same problem again, when the guy I'm with isn't even human? What the hell kind of pattern is that?"

"Matthew? What pattern?"

I spun on a heel and waved a finger at him. "This. You. How did I end up with a *dragon* who's afraid of commitment? How could I possibly be this kind of unlucky? I'm dating outside my fucking species, for fuck's sake. I really am broken, or cursed, or something. I must be. Hell, there are dragons, and Templars, and magic—maybe I am literally cursed."

Reece stood hesitantly. "Matthew, I am not afraid of what claiming you means for me—I'm afraid of what it means for *you*, and our son."

I laughed, full on, a belly aching, nervous-breakdown kind of laugh. "You know what's hilarious? I've actually heard that exact thing before, except in plain English. Rex said it—my ex—except when he said that it was 'I love you, baby, but I'm bad for you. It'll be better this way, I don't deserve to be loved.' Doesn't matter what species you are, apparently it's all about you assholes. And then Thomas, and Manny who both didn't want to be committed so they didn't limit *my* options, it's some kind of fucking—"

Reece took me by my shoulders and kissed me. I wanted to resist, to tell him that kissing me wouldn't change anything but honestly... it did. I calmed, and not because of some kind of magic—there was no rush of warmth, no swell of calm that took me over. It was just him, and me, and that kiss. Its own kind of magic, maybe.

"You have to see how crazy that is," I whispered when he gave me space to breathe. "Reece... if there's any chance that I could be taken away from you, or whatever, then you have to know that given the choice I would choose you and a tent under a bridge. I don't care what's coming for us, as long as this family is intact."

The moment I said it, a sense of certainty settled over me. I calmed the rest of the way, and chuckled as my eyes stung. I put a hand on my belly, then took Reece's and put it there as well. I gazed up at him. "I'm your mate, Reece. And you're mine. What more do either of us need?"

"My mate," he rasped. His fingers dug gently into my stomach, as if he could reach inside and caress our unborn child. "My child. My family."

I nodded, and pressed close to Reece. "Claim me, Reece. Make me yours. Forever. Whatever happens, it happens to both of us. I'm not afraid."

Chapter 24
Matthew

Whatever I expected, it wasn't what happened. Telling Reece to claim me pulled some trigger, unleashed something that had been barely coiled beneath the surface of him. He growled like an animal as he scooped me up and carried me from the tent in his arms.

People noticed.

He marched to our camper, and only put me down when the door was open. He urged me up the steps and inside, and locked the door behind us. The next thing I knew, he was tearing my clothes off. The cotton of my shirt tore, and he tossed the resulting rag behind him as he nudged me toward the bed. When I bumped into the edge, my stomach fluttering with fear and excitement, he gave my cargo shorts the same treatment, impatient to have me naked.

His own clothes went next and with about as much care for whether they were wearable afterward—I supposed he could just shift himself some new ones—and then he was on top of me, spreading my knees to get between my thighs, and waves of heat radiated between us.

"You want this?" he asked as he bit at my neck.

"Yes," I gasped. "I want it. Reece… make me yours, baby. Claim me."

Another of those animal sounds rumbled through him, and under my hands where I clawed at the muscles of his back, his skin grew coarser, ridged like the ghost of scales. His body rippled against mine, vibrating as a small fire seemed to ignite under his skin.

"Then I do claim you, Matthew Stiles," he rasped, his voice a mix of draconian and human, "as my mate. Now and for all time. I place my mark upon you, that all shall know to whom you belong, and to whom I am promised, in this age and the next."

With that said, he heaved himself upright and drew me with him. His face had changed as well, to a mix of dragon and man, his lips hardened, his eyes burning bright. I had a moment of fear at the sudden change in his appearance but when he opened his mouth to show sharp teeth some instinct inside me told me precisely what I was meant to do. I bent my neck to expose it and my shoulder to him, and reached up to pull his head to me.

The pain was brief. His teeth sank into the flesh of my shoulder, just to the side of my neck, but almost the moment I winced at the hurt it was replaced by a flood of heat that spread quickly to every part of my body. It coursed through my veins, burned in my loins, set my limbs tingling and gave me a rush like I'd never felt before. A hunger for him took me over, like something physical had reached into me and pulled something out, placing it inside Reece for safekeeping and all I could think of was becoming one with him—merging until this exchange became a true union.

When he released me, his body had changed back to one that was purely human, his cock pressed against mine, both of us painfully hard. I knew it, too—I could feel some new dimension to myself that was an echo of his. I rocked my hips, grinding against him, and felt the smoothness of my own skin and the spark of pleasure that jolted through Reece's cock.

And I felt the heat of his desire for me, rushing back and forth between us, magnifying itself, until I couldn't see straight and all I knew was Reece's tongue in my mouth, his hands traveling over my skin and mine over his. He grunted as he hunched against me, and slick fluid spread between us.

Without warning, he broke our kiss and hauled me over onto my stomach. Strong hands gripped my hips and pulled them up from the bed until I had my ass in the air, and before I could so much as beg him to fill me, his slippery, hot coal of a tongue speared me, his hands pulling at me as if he could get further inside that way.

I howled as the thick muscle teased my hole and sent embers of crippling pleasure scattering over my nerves, into my gut, and down to the tip of my weeping cock. He devoured me without mercy, and dug his fingers almost painfully into my inner hip as he did. My nerves overloaded, gave up all control, and all I could do was mewl into my pillow. I wailed his name, or tried to—all that came out were more muffled moans. My legs shook, and when he bit one cheek to give my hungry ring a break, I cried out and twisted my torso against his grip. It didn't hurt—far from it; the shock of it simply drove my body to act on its own.

A rough hand pushed between my thighs to find my cock. Reece's hand was already slick from something, and when he gripped my cock tight and milked down slowly, I nearly levitated off the bed. His fist caught the head of my dick and twisted cruelly, one way and then the other, until I reached down with one hand to claw at his hand. "Too much," I begged, "fuck, Reece, it's too much, please, baby, fuck me…"

All that I got in response was a dark, low chuckle of approval and more of the overwhelming treatment, until I could barely breathe and every moan became a whimper of helpless need for him to finish me, make me come for him. I was so close when he stopped that I gave a plaintive wail of disappointment, and looked down at him with wet eyes. "No, no—I was so close, Reece, make me—"

The next thing I felt was the pressure of his cock pressing against my hole, and then the weight of his body as he bent over me and hooked his hand under my chin. He lifted my head and pressed his lips to my ear. "You can feel me, yes?"

I swiveled my hips, trying to press him into my aching, empty hole, to be complete again, but he was careful to move with me. "I can," I moaned. "I can feel you, baby, please…"

"Not this," he said, and gave a gentle thrust that slipped the head of him inside. "More. We are bonded. Feel me. Seek me out—the new place in your heart. Look for it…"

At that very moment, all I could feel was the nearness of him, and the tease of his cock promising to fill me up but not yet making good on it. Still, I turned my attention inward as he murmured to me, and that heat that he had spread into me before seemed to reach up and meet me halfway. It was a calm, throbbing, steady flame—and something more. Like an echo in vast chamber, both right there in my ear and coming from someplace far away. From all around me.

"That is me, my mate," Reece breathed against my ear as he pressed forward, thrusting slowly into me. "That is my heart, beating with yours. That is my love, Matthew. Feel…"

With that word, he sank into me completely, and I arched my back to slam him all the way inside. I was swallowed up in the fire, and once I knew what it was I could only feel the truth of it. I pulled Reece's arms around me, and he rolled us onto our sides. While I clutched at the hand beneath me, his free hand traveled down my exposed side and pulled my leg back to tangle with his and then found my cock. He stroked me slowly, in time with his patient but urgent thrusting. His teeth grazed my neck, my earlobe, and his warm breath tickled my skin, his tongue darting out to tease me. I closed my eyes to keep the world from spinning, and heaved heavy, ragged breaths as the dual sensations of my pleasure and his swirled and tangled inside.

"You will join me," Reece rasped, and his fist moved faster over my shaft, twisting when it found the head of my cock, as if he meant to wring my climax out of me by gentle force. "Come with me, Matthew. Give yourself to me."

His knot swelled. My prostate sent a stampede of fresh new agonies through every muscle. I sucked in a breath, clawed at Reece's arm and hip, and froze like I'd been turned to stone when he bit my neck hard, and gave my cock a final, languid twist.

Reece slammed his hips forward, his knot thumped against my gland, and his cock gushed inside me. His orgasm echoed into me, and I jerked against his teeth on my neck as my own hit me twice as hard. He held tight to my dick as it sent pulse after pulse of cum over his fingers, onto the bed. My ass clenched as I pumped more out, squeezing Reece's knot. The pressure send a fresh new cascade of pleasure along his body that I could feel like a second skin of my own, and when he jettisoned another gush of seed into me, I shot again, weaker but more intense.

All I could do was gasp like a fish on a rock as he continued to milk me slowly and fill me up. Every new explosion spread through me like my own, and I knew that the same reflections were cascading through him when my spent cock reacted in kind. By the time this passing back-and-forth of mini-orgasms was done, I had twisted enough to kiss him, but we'd both become so transfixed by the exchange that we no longer kissed actively—we simply held position, trading breath, shuddering with each aftershock until they grew far enough apart that only the deep, peaceful glow was left.

We floated in that for what seemed like an endless age of sweet nothingness, tied together, his knot holding fasted inside me, pulsing only slightly every few minutes.

It took hours and a short nap before I came back to myself and felt the knot abating. It was like having my heart removed. The moment it was gone, I moaned a senseless complaint and tried to nudge my hips back against him. "Stay in," I whined softly. "Stay with me, Reece."

He pushed back in but only for a moment before he withdrew carefully. "I cannot. It will take time to contact my friend. The sooner I leave, the sooner I can return."

I twisted in his arms, and pulled his lips to mine. His kiss was sweet and long, and happened in slow motion. "Do you have to go?"

"It is the best way," he said, his nose brushing mine. "But I will return. You have my promise. We are bound now. You bear my mark, on your body and in your very soul. I bear you with me in kind. We cannot be separated by distance, my mate, nor by time or perhaps even death. You will be safe here with Joseph and his people to look over you."

"He isn't you," I said.

"No," Reece agreed. "But his people are fierce, and strong, and in numbers they are every bit as dangerous. You will be safe, whatever happens."

"And will you?" I asked.

His lip twitched, amused as he pulled me close and nuzzled my hair. "I am a dragon."

"My dragon," I murmured. Exhaustion caught up with me, my body spent. Our mixed scent seemed to coalesce around me, and was strangely comforting in a way it never was before. "Stay with me until I fall asleep?"

He nodded against me, and scooted down a bit so that I could lay my head on his chest, his strong arm tight around my shoulders. "Sleep, my love. Be at peace."

At least for that moment, maybe for the first time in my life—I really, truly was.

Chapter 25
Reece

Claiming one's mate is an experience regarded as utterly private. As such, my own sire and broodmother, one of the last females of my kind, never told me what the experience truly was. Now, I knew—and a part of me wished that I had waited until my return to claim Matthew.

His kisses were sweeter. The joining of our bodies was deeper, and left traces that haunted me the moment we were parted. There was a new presence in my chest, as if some part of him were lodged there and could never be removed. It did, however, feel the strain of distance.

I took flight that night, after dark, from the desert. Joseph accompanied us, so that Matthew could see me off, and the moment I left the ground and beat my wings to reach the sky, it was as though a steel chain were tied to my heart and staked to the ground. It was painful to leave him. Joseph's favors were answered, and his people were around the camp. Matthew would be safe, I knew—the pain was not merely one of concern, but seemingly physical.

It did not let up as I sped north and west, back to the city to find Tarin. Where exactly the outcasts nested, I didn't know. Somewhere in the Rocky Mountains, but that was a large territory to comb and I did not have the leisure of boundless time. Concealed from watchful eyes, I flew as high above the clouds as I dared, seeking the ideal altitude where the air was thin enough not to impede me, but still able to hold me aloft. Though I hungered, I dared not stop until Portland was in sight.

The journey took most of a day. When at last the sun set again, I used the cover of darkness to plunge through the clouds and seek out one of the small islands that dotted the Columbia River, and from there slipped into the frigid water the same way I had left the city to pursue Matthew. When I again emerged this time, it was in my human skin, in a soaking gray suit that I summoned a bit of my fire to dry out.

"So it's true then," Tarin said, once I had contacted him and arranged the meeting. For Matthew's sake, I met Tarin at the bar where he'd pointed my mate out to me, intent on delivering a message to Yuri on Matthew's behalf afterward. Tarin gave a low whistle, and sipped something that smelled like it could clean scales quite effectively. "And you went and took him for yourself."

I glowered at my outcast friend. "It did not precisely occur the way you suggest."

"Call it however you like," he said, grinning. "I promise not to tell."

"Your discretion is not my concern," I said. "My concern now is only for Matthew's safety, and the survival of our people. What could the Templars possibly want with the bones of one of our females?"

Tarin blew out a long breath, blinking slowly as he considered the matter. "Honestly? I'm not entirely sure. But I know someone who might. One of my people was outcast close to three thousand years ago. He's got a couple of kids, as well. Doesn't see 'em, and that was a long time ago, but he might know a thing or two about dragon births. Not sure he ever made with one of the sacred omegas, but he knows a lot about a lot. I could put you in touch."

"Could you send him to Texas? I do not precisely have unlimited time to wait."

"Guess not," Tarin grunted. "Well… there are only a couple of passages that way without pissing anybody off. But if I leave tonight, I can get a message to him, and if he can leave right away it'll take him maybe three days? He'll have to go east first. Bristrix and his brood run a big chunk of the Midwest, and they keep an eye on the skies there. And we can't even look in the general direction of Arizona without getting sternly worded messages from Nemrood's folks."

Three days. I mulled that with some consternation, but while I could ask Tarin to lobby on my behalf, I certainly couldn't expect any of the outcasts to put their lives in danger for me, or for Matthew. Not until or unless I became one of them.

"You know if the elders hear about this, you're fucked, right?" Tarin asked.

I emerged from my thoughts to nod thoughtfully. "It is all but inevitable."

"Is it worth it?" he asked, this time with a hint of what I could only call wistfulness. "Claiming a mate? Having a youngling on the way? What's it like?"

My creeping smile was entirely involuntary. "Nothing like I imagined it would be. Even now, I could turn and point to him, and there is a powerful pressure to return to him. Being with him… it is like we are one life, spread between two bodies. And there is some feeling between us. A deep, aching sort of… love."

"You sure that's what it is?" Tarin pressed.

I nodded. "Yes. I could not have defined it before, but something about the process—the claiming—it's as though whole new spectrums of emotion are open to me. I can't even describe them all. But I know that one without doubt."

The outcast dragon leaned back in his seat and studied his drink. "I always wondered. Well. If I'm gonna get you the help you need, I should leave. It's a long drive."

"If you were to tell me where—"

"No," he said firmly, shaking his head as he stood and collected his jacket. "No, they'd never speak to me again if I sent you out there. We value our privacy, you know? And even if I'm stuck like this, they're still the only people I've got. Them and you. Once all the dust settles, you come to me and I'll make introductions. We may not have the same rigid sense of bureaucracy and blind obedience, but, you know—we're family all the same somehow."

I took his joke on the chin, and tipped my glass of water to him. "I suppose I'll find out."

He paused at the edge of the table after he'd slipped his arms into his jacket and zipped it up. "Hey, Reece?"

"Mm?"

Tarin rubbed his jaw. "You know… there are probably more like Matthew out there."

I bobbed my head. "I suspect that's the case. Even if only distant cousins from the same bloodline."

"Well," Tarin said, "what if... what if it was just us? Outcasts, I mean. And you'll be one of us soon enough. What if instead of telling the elders and ancients about this—what if we kept it to ourselves. This world is changed, brother. I'm not so sure the old ways are the best ways anymore. Those of us that got thrown out, we've had to adapt, grow, survive in a changing world. It just might be we're the better people to take care of our future."

"Tarin, I don't—"

He waved my words away. "Just think about it, okay? I'm not saying we go to war. Just that if we had some advantage, maybe things would finally change. Be careful out there. Take care of your mate."

I didn't need to answer that, and Tarin didn't expect it. He patted the table, and turned to leave. I gave his words some serious consideration as he did, and for some time after he was gone, before finally leaving the bar myself to go and give Matthew's friend his message.

Matthew's instructions were easy enough to follow. I pressed the button for his apartment, and almost immediately a familiar voice answered. "Yes? Who is it?"

"A friend of Matthew's," I replied.

There was a long pause. "What friend? Who are you?"

"We've met once before," I said. "At the bar downstairs."

There was no other response.

I buzzed again, and waited, but it seemed that Yuri wanted nothing to do with me. Matthew had asked that I persist, however, so I pressed the button twice more before there was movement beyond the glass door.

Yuri stalked toward me through the hallway. He had his phone in one hand. When he reached the door, he cracked it just enough that we could speak. I took a step back, sensing from the look on his face that he did not entirely trust me. "Okay, talk. I have got my finger on the dial for 911, just so you know. What do you know about Matt?"

"Matthew is in Texas," I said. "He is safe. Due to circumstances beyond his control, his phone was lost, and he has not been able to recover it. I had business here, and he sent me to tell you that he is well, and that he wishes he could reach out. Where he is there is no access to the internet, and he... he does not know your number. He told me to convey to you, as a means of proving that I do speak for him, that—you must forgive my incivility—that your 'gift' is pretty shit if it could not foresee the kind of fuckery he has had to put up with since he left."

Yuri narrowed his eyes at me. "He said this?"

I nodded.

Yuri put his phone away reluctantly, and pushed the door the rest of the way open. "So. You went with him to Texas?"

"Yes," I said. It was easier that way.

"I called his hotel, you know," he said. "They say he left his room a mess. As if someone had tossed the place."

"We left in something of a hurry," I said. "I did attempt to make the room as presentable as was possible."

"He could not go to a town and use a computer at a library, perhaps?" Yuri pressed. I realized that where he was worried before, now he was hurt. His eyes glossed, and he looked away to wipe them. "Is he safe? Are you two…?"

"We are," I said. "But I assure you, I am not withholding him from you. There is a situation that is… complicated. He wishes that you could be with him in his current trials."

Yuri snorted softly and squinted up at me. "Has he told you that you have a very strange way of speaking?"

I laughed. "As a matter of fact, yes, he has. On more than one occasion."

Yuri hmphed, and leaned against the door. "Okay. And he is safe?"

"He is," I confirmed. "But… he may be some time before he can return here. He merely wanted that I should assure you that he is not, I believe his words were, 'dead in a ditch' somewhere."

"Good," Yuri said. "Tell him, I will come to him. The semester is over. I will go to Catarina and meet him there."

"That may not be the best—" I started.

Yuri stepped back, and let the door close. He nodded once, and then turned to march back up the hallway, disappearing around a corner at the far end.

Immediately, I regretted bringing Matthew's friend word of his safety. But there was no time to work out how I might convince him to stay here, where he was out of harm's way. I had a mate to return to, and an ancient dragon skeleton to somehow keep out of the hands of Templars.

I turned to leave, and something gripped my heart and squeezed. Terror flooded me, so powerful that I nearly shifted on the street to take flight. When I realized that the terror was not my own, it was only compounded.

Matthew. It was my mate's fear, reaching across the distance between us.

Heedless of onlookers, I sprinted down the street until I found a gap between buildings. I dashed into the darkness, shifted to the smallest form I could managed, and leapt to catch the air as I concealed myself.

I knew, though, that it was not possible to reach him in time to stop what was already happening.

Chapter 26
Matthew

I woke to the sound of howling wolves. At first it was only one, barely stirring me awake. Then there were more. In a moment, it seemed that the howling came from all directions. A chill ran through me, and I sat bolt upright, my heart already racing. Something was wrong.

Seconds later, the door opened. I scrambled toward the wall of the camper behind me, relaxing only marginally when Joseph leapt up the steps. He spotted me, and held a hand out. "Come on. They're here, and they're coming in force. We were wrong."

"They're here for me?" I asked, panicked and unable to make my body move. I saw flashes of steel in my mind's eye, and this time the instinct to fight or flee was better informed but no less crippling in the moment.

"And the bones," he said. "There are too many for just you. Matt, we gotta get you out of here. I promised Reece I'd keep you safe. Get dressed, they're close."

I shook my head. "I c-can't... I c-can't move, I—"

Joseph came the rest of the way into the camper and grabbed clothes at random from the suitcase. He held them in one hand and offered me the other when he came to the edge of the bed. "I know you must be scared," he said. "I promised Reece I would keep you safe, and that's what I'm going to do until he gets back. Give me your hand, Matt. You have to think about that baby."

Of course, I did. I was. But hearing it out loud seemed to break whatever invisible bonds of neurology locked my limbs tight. I nodded quickly, and forced my legs to move first, then crawled to the edge and took his hand. He helped me up, and looked away as I dressed.

"We're gonna go east, out into the desert. You got good shoes?"

"Under the seat by the suitcase," I said as I pulled a pair of jeans on.

Joseph retrieved them and tossed them to me, then disappeared back through the door. I dressed as quickly as I could, and then stumbled down the steps to meet him.

He tugged me toward the east end of camp but I pulled back. "Mercy," I breathed. "We have to bring her with us. We have to get everyone out of here, we can't just let them—"

Joseph turned on me, "Mercy is already gone, I sent her ahead."

"And the others?" I insisted.

"They're not my responsibility," he hissed. "You are, and I can't get all of them out of here without drawing attention. We'll leave tracks, they'll hunt us down. Now come on, you have to think about yourself and your child."

He started to pull me along but I couldn't make myself turn my back on everyone in camp. If the Templars were coming to cut them all down and clean up after themselves, everyone here would be killed. I jerked my hand out of Joseph's and turned toward Professor Taylor's tent.

I heard Joseph running after me, but when he didn't tackle me to the ground, I ignored the sound of his boots on the dirt and threw open Taylor's tent flap.

"Professor, you have to…"

He wasn't there. His tent was wrecked, though, and as I took a step back something squished under my heel. I looked down to see that the rugs over the floor of the place were soaked.

Blood.

Oh, fuck.

I turned away from the scene, and Joseph's hand clamped down on my wrist. I swung at him with my free hand, but he was faster, and caught that wrist mid-swing. He had a look of resignation on his face. "Stop. You can't win this."

"You fucking—"

"Quiet," he snapped, and pulled me out of the tent and into the open air. "Look. I'm sorry, but Reece's people aren't the only ones in the crosshairs, and they aren't what they used to be. My people are at risk, too. We gotta cut deals. We can't just hide in mountains or turn invisible or take to the sky when shit gets bad."

"He trusted you," I ground out as I struggled to get free. I kicked, but he blocked it with his knee and left me with a shin that felt like it had nearly broken in the exchange. "I trusted you. Where is Mercy?"

"I don't know," he said, and jerked me off balance. I stumbled, and he let go of one wrist to move smoothly around me and pin one arm behind my back. He gave it a tug when I started to lunge forward, and the pain stopped me cold. He pulled me against him and growled into my ear. "That's the truth, all right? I think she ran when she heard Taylor."

"Taylor's dead," I said. "There was blood. Did you do it?"

Joseph didn't answer. He gave me a shove, just enough to get me moving, and grabbed a fistful of hair. "I really wish it could be different. But trust me. They would have found you eventually."

Cold poured into my stomach as I realized that even if I did get away from Joseph, there was nowhere to go. I couldn't sprint across twenty miles of desert to the nearest town. He marched me out past the campers, away from the dim lights that felt at least marginally like safety, and into a darkness that I knew would be where I died.

Reece. You have to make it back. You have to come for me.

I could feel him, distantly, like the point of a compass inside was always pointed toward him now. But I could also tell he was a long way off.

Too far to make it in time.

All I could think about as the darkness engulfed us was my baby. And what I would do to make sure we both survived.

Chapter 27
Matthew

We walked some distance from camp. I don't know how far, but it was a walk. Why, I didn't know, so I asked.

"You worried about the diggers," Joseph said. "Witnesses would have to be dealt with."

"Then what happened to Taylor?" I demanded. "He didn't see anything, why kill him?"

Joseph sighed. "Why do you think?"

I didn't dignify the question with an answer, but I thought I knew. Taylor wasn't going to let them box up the bones and close up shop. He must have had plans to tell someone. I had the horrible thought that Mercy must have known, and that she was part of all this—but Joseph had no reason to tell me that she'd fled if she was involved. Maybe she was out here in the darkness. And secretly a ninja. She did have a remarkable list of pseudo-professions.

Before I had much time to decide whether Mercy was coming to my rescue or not, the dark silhouette of a Hummer came into view. Joseph pushed me toward it. I resisted, but all that got me was a knuckle in my back and a painfully twisted ankle.

"Joseph," I begged, "please don't do this. Think of my baby, please—"

"I'm thinking of my children," he said flatly. "And those of my siblings and cousins."

"And you think these people are going to just turn a blind eye to your people if you fuck mine?" I tried to stomp his foot, tangle him up, anything, but something told me this wasn't the first time Joseph had frog-marched someone. The Hummer got closer and closer.

"Your people, are they?" He gave a humorless chuckle. "You've got no idea what they'd do to you, kid. They aren't your people. You're as much of a criminal as Reece is. Believe me, getting rid of the dragons is a good thing. Especially after what they did to us. You don't know what they're like, you just know your mate."

"And so do you," I growled as I dug my heels in. "You know he's not going let you off easy for this just because you've got some kind of beef with dragons. You really want an angry dragon after you?"

"The thing you're forgetting," Joseph said as the door to the Hummer opened, "is who wiped out half the dragons in the world before they stole our omegas and turned them into concubines. Go."

He let me go, but positioned himself so that if I ran it would be easy to stop me. I rubbed my wrists, and peered at the open door. No one had gotten out, and there was no execution squad. But that could just mean they intended to do it inside. Still, no one emerged to drag me inside. I glanced back at Joseph, but he just waved me on.

I crept around the edge of the door, squinting into the darkness for some sign of a gun, or knife. Instead, I saw the dim light inside. The windows were blacked out, and a man sat inside, his hands draped over the handle of a cane. He was older, his hair silvering at the sides, and there were deep frown lines spreading from the corners of a sour mouth. He was heavyset, and one hand was scarred. Burns, I thought.

I waited at the threshold. "Who are you? What do you want with me?"

The man gestured at the seat across from him. "To talk, and answer both of those questions, Matthew. Come. Have a seat."

I did not 'have a seat'. "The last time I saw your people, they were trying to kill me."

The man tilted his head a bit, and the corner of his mouth tugged up. "Well, things have changed since then, now haven't they. Hm?" He raised the end of his cane and pointed at my abdomen.

I put a protective hand over my stomach. Joseph, of course. He'd told them.

"You've got no place to run," the man said. "At least if you're in here with me, you've got a fighting chance. I'm an old man, and I'm in here alone. I haven't fought my own battles in person for many years."

Joseph still stood behind me. There was really only the one choice, so I resigned myself to it and stepped up into the vehicle. When I did, the man gave Joseph a nod, and he closed the door behind me as I slid onto the seat in the opposite corner from the Templar.

"So," I said. "I'm here. Who are you?"

"My name," he said, "is Hugh de Payens. I lead the Holy Order of the Knights Templar in its current iteration. And there are things you should know about your... friend."

"My mate," I corrected. "Who you should think twice about fucking with."

Hugh showed his teeth in a broad, vicious smile. "Oh. I'm adept at 'fucking' with his kind. For starters, rule number one is always: if you get the mate, you get the dragon. So you have my thanks for getting knocked up. It will make it that much easier to put another dragon hide in my collection."

I ground my teeth, and tried to decide if he was lying or not. Reece would come for me—he already was; I could feel it. But how did someone like Hugh, or even an army of people like him, pose any threat to a dragon? I had seen Reece—he was mammoth. He had magic and fire. "How do you kill a dragon?"

He chuckled, and tapped the side of his nose. "You've got a ways to go with the interrogation skills. You'll find out. Let me ask you this in the meantime. How much has your 'mate' told you about his people? What they're like, what they do. What they've done in the past. You know that baby's history?"

"I know your people hunted them." Joseph's words echoed in my mind. That they'd *stolen* omegas. "That you slaughtered their females to try and drive them to extinction."

Hugh's head bobbed slowly. "Both of those things are true. But do you know *why*?"

I didn't. So I didn't answer.

Hugh didn't seem to mind. "Dragons are old. Older than us by a lot. And you might think they're some remnant from the Jurassic Age, but you'd be wrong. They're not dinosaurs, kid. They're not from here at all. See, there are all kinds of worlds out there beyond this one. All mashed up together like a pile of papers. Something happened back in the sheet of paper they came from, and they skipped town and came here. And wouldn't you know, our sheet was chock full of tasty varmints. Except, we were good for more than eating. Ever hear stories about dragons demanding treasure, and virgin princesses?"

I shrugged. "Propaganda?"

He drummed his fingers once on the handle of his cane. "Dragons are predators," he said darkly. "Do you really think they came here and decided to live in peace and harmony? You saw Jurassic Park, right? Course you did."

I knew Reece. I knew he wasn't a predator. Not in the sense Hugh meant it, at least. Didn't I? A quiet kind of doubt nibbled at the back of my head. I *didn't* know anything about Reece's people. I just knew the one dragon. Maybe he was an exception. "You're just trying to get into my head."

De Payens shrugged, not really denying it. "Maybe. Or maybe it's just the truth and the truth is a little ugly. Joseph tell you about how your lover's people solved their breeding crisis?"

"Joseph isn't exactly high on my list of trusted sources at this point," I said. Hugh didn't respond, but raised a bushy eyebrow. The silence grew awkward enough that I spoke almost involuntarily. "He… says that the dragons stole omegas."

"Stole them and changed them," Hugh replied. "Worked their magic on your ancestors' bodies, made them into concubines."

I shook my head. "No. There was an agreement. They helped Reece's people survive."

"Did they now?" He chuckled softly. "Come on. You don't know the first thing about the Wolven, do you? 'Cause I do. And I can tell you that their omegas are precious to them. Revered like a gift from their pagan wolf-god. A special gift, just for them. You really think they gave up their most treasured assets to be farmed like little baby factories just so the dragons—who may as well be immortal from our point of view—could make a few new lizard-whelps?"

"I'm not turning on Reece," I said finally, and folded my arms. "It doesn't matter what you say. It doesn't matter to me what happened in the past. Humans aren't blameless or bloodless either. We've committed genocide, we've enslaved each other, we've destroyed nations—we still do it. So even if everything you're saying is true, it doesn't change anything. We all fight to survive and sometimes other people get hurt in the process. We move on and do better, and that's the same for everyone. I love Reece. He loves me. I don't know what you think you're going to get by trying to make me hate him or his people but you're not getting it."

Hugh pursed his lips, and sagged back in his seat, one finger tapping slowly on the handle of his cane as he looked me over as if weighing options or deciding what size clothing I wore. Finally he shrugged one shoulder and smiled. "Boy, I don't need you to turn. What I need from you won't require your cooperation anyway. Just time, and patience, and when the time comes a sharp scalpel and a hole in the ground."

I know that I went pale, because every part of me grew ice cold.

"Better settle in," he said. "It's a long flight from Portland to Texas. We've got a bit of a wait ahead of us."

Chapter 28
Reece

By the time I saw the red and brown sprawl of land around the dig site again, it was dusk. I had changed midair on the way, taking on my full size to move faster, and the effort of both that change and the long journey had left me starving. I sailed over the camp, searching with eyes and heart for Matthew, and sensed him nearby when I spotted a glint of metallic black in the distance, almost two miles from the dig.

Passing over the camp, I caught the faint scent of blood.

Matthew was alive, but whether he was harmed or not, I couldn't tell. He was still afraid, but not only that—there was fierce determination coming across our bond as well. As I closed in on a line of three parked vehicles, all black with windows darkened to the point that not even my eyes could see through them, I almost expected to find him fighting for his life.

They were waiting for me. Almost certainly, this meant that there was some trap set. Templars had no end of tricks for luring and trapping my people. I saw no lanes, no ballistae—none of the old tools—but that did not mean it was safe. Knowing that, however, did not change what I had to do.

I tucked my wings close, pressed my legs against my body tighter, and shot toward the ground like an arrow. Just shy of the ground, I snapped my wings out with the crack of thunder and alighted on the earth. Though still concealed, the claw marks on the ground and the cloud of sand and dust that my wings created were enough to give me away. Hiding, though, would be pointless and indeed, when men poured out of the three vehicles, they did not look confused.

One of them was de Payens. He waved to the inside of his boxy vehicle, and my heart thudded against my chest when Matthew emerged, as if it were trying to leap out of me and run to him.

"Show yourself," de Payens called. "We all know you're there and where you are. Why not awe us with your majesty?"

"Release my mate," I bellowed, "or every one of you will burn."

Of the eight men assembled, all but de Payens took several steps back. De Payens only turned to grab Matthew by the wrist, and jerked him off balance. Matthew struggled, and managed to strike the man in the face with one elbow, but de Payens ignored the blow and pulled the top of his cane free to reveal a slender dagger. He whipped it up to press against Matthew's throat.

"No!" The ground shook with my roar.

"Out in the open," de Payens called. "There are more of my people out there. I kill your mate, you burn us all—I still ensure one less generation of lizards. It's a win for us no matter what, dragon."

My claws curled slowly into the earth, tearing up foot-deep furrows. Matthew's fear and fury coursed through me, but the fear was beginning to win in him. "Do not harm him," I said quieter, though some still flinched to hear my voice.

I unraveled the concealment, and tucked my wings closed.

Some of the Templars gathered had not seen a dragon before. All but three of them began to shake visibly, and the smell of their fear sweat found me on the slight breeze. I swept my eyes among them, and mentally marked the ones that didn't show their fear, and then glared down at their leader. "Let him go, de Payens. I beg you. Halt this senseless killing. My people live in hiding. Let us continue in peace and secrecy."

"For now," he said. "Sure. But when there are more of you? When you start breeding again, and your population grows, and you all decide maybe the old ways are best after all? This isn't a battle for the present, beast. It's a war for the future. You and yours don't belong here. Now. You put yourself in a more manageable form, or I cut the boy."

"Reece, no," Matthew barked. De Payens pressed the blade harder against his throat. I smelled my mate's blood—just drops, but enough that rage nearly took me over. And would have, if not for my fear for Matthew's life.

"Quiet," de Payens growled.

Matthew's face twisted with fury. He met my eyes, and a powerful rush of conviction poured across our bond. "Reece," he said, snarling as de Payens threatened to cut him again, "*dracarys*."

I… tried to hide my confusion. Matthew raised his eyebrows, clearly suggesting something, but the feelings I received from him were as confusing as what he'd said. Without understanding clearly what he wanted, my only choice was to give de Payens what he demanded.

With a breath, I shifted out of my true form and into my human body, dressed in clothing similar to the men with guns. If there was going to be a fight, looking like one of them was ideal. I put my hands up as I approached de Payens. "Here I am," I said. "Now please. Release Matthew, and I'll go with you, do whatever you require."

"I just bet you would," de Payens said. "Lock him down, boys."

Men circled around the vehicles and converged on me. I kept my eyes on de Payens and my mate as they bound my wrists in heavy metal shackles. Something in the metal stung my skin, spreading an itch down into my palms and up my arms to my elbows. Serpentine, set into the shackles. I gritted my teeth at the burn. Shifting back into my dragon form would be impossible as long as they were on.

De Payens, however, did keep his unspoken end of the bargain. He took the blade away from Matthew's throat. "There. So much easier when you cooperate, isn't it? Now, I promise you—your mate is perfectly safe. I'll see to it your whelp is born. After all—he can teach us a lot more about your kind."

I roared and lurched forward to plow into de Payens, intent on killing him with my human teeth if I needed to, but thunder exploded at the back of my head, and the world winked out of existence.

I came to in the darkness with a gasp, and tried instinctively to reach for the throbbing pain at the back of my skull. My hand didn't make it far, and the world resolved itself gradually as my head cleared. I was on the ground, spread-eagle. Legs and wrists chained. I was weak, as well, my body chilled. I craned my neck, and became aware of a persistent, sharp pain at my elbow. There was a needle in my arm, and a tube ascending from one end of it to a small bag dangling from a squat metal contraption near my waist. Already, four of the bags were full. There were still five empty. Some distance past my feet, a barbed metal lance leaned against the remaining vehicle. The other two had gone. Matthew was some distance away already. Still alive.

Two of the Templars stood a short distance from the lance. "...and she makes this lasagna just like my grandma's. Think I might take her to meet my parents."

"Seriously," the other one said. "Getting serious. Never thought I'd see the day."

"Yeah, she's gonna be pissed when I get back," the first muttered. "How long before this lizard is dry? I need to get back to cell service. The boss could have told us this was gonna take a few days."

"Be glad you're not hauling bones," his companion said. "You see those things? Jesus, they're huge. You have any idea they were that big?"

There was no answer to that, but a second later the two of them stiffened. "You hear that?"

"Yeah... keep an eye on the lizard. Probably just one of those fucking dog men prowling around."

One of the two peeled off to hunt down the source of the sound. I strained to hear with human ears, but they weren't sharp enough to track footsteps or determine what it was the guard heard.

I did, however, catch some small movement at the back of the vehicle. When I focused on it, a silhouette in the darkness raised a hand and gestured at me. *Stay down*.

There wasn't much of a choice, but I lowered my head back to the ground carefully, and tried not to let the tension in my body rattle the chains the bound me. I waited. Dirt crunched.

"Christ, you scared—who the fuck are y—"

The remaining Templar's words cut off with a crunch and a woman's grunt of effort. I lifted my head again to get a look just as he collapsed. His attacker dropped something heavy, and put her hands to her mouth. "Oh, Goddess... oh, I'm so sorry, that was so much worse than I thought it would be."

"Mercy?" I whispered.

She shook her hands out and trotted to me. "Reece! What are they doing?"

"Taking my blood," I said flatly. "You must free me. They have Matthew, I need to go after him. Be quick, there is another Templar around."

"I know," she whispered as she twisted the shackle around, "I threw a rock. Works in movies so... these things are locked."

"Keys, probably on the guard," I said.

Mercy scrambled back to the guard and continued to mutter apologies as she dug through his pockets. A moment of searching and she gave a soft hoot of victory, and rushed back to me to start unlocking the shackles. She got both ankles and one wrist before the other guard returned. He gave one look to us, one to his fallen comrade, and then drew a pistol and trained it on Mercy.

"Stop what you're doing and drop the keys!"

Mercy froze for half a second, then jammed the key into the lock and turned it.

The Templar fired.

Mercy cried out in pain just as I surged forward. I spread my fingers, expecting them to become claws, but the shift wouldn't happen. Instead, I plowed into the Templar and bowled him over. We struggled over the gun. Two shots fired into the night before I managed to curl his arm under my own and twist hard to one side. Bone broke. The pistol dropped from his grip. I smashed my elbow into his face. His cheek first, then his jaw, and finally his temple before he stopped struggling.

As I struggled to my feet, the other Templar groaned. I kicked him in the face as I strode toward Mercy, and knelt by her side when I got to her. "You are injured."

"Yes," she said, her voice trembling as she pressed a hand to her arm. "He shot me. It, um, it really hurts. Hoo, boy. I think it went all the way through. That's gonna need medical attention, I don't think crystals are going to fix this."

I scooped up the keys from the dirt, and slipped a hand under her uninjured arm to help her to her feet. "Keep pressure on the wound. We will take their vehicle. Matthew is with their leader, we must move quickly."

Mercy nodded as she stood, and breathed sharply as I led her to the car. As she got in, I tore open one of the Templars' uniforms and ripped his shirt away. When I seated myself in the driver's side, and handed the material to Mercy. "Use this to stem the bleeding. And I highly recommend utilizing the seatbelt. This is going to be a rather uncomfortable ride."

Chapter 29
Matthew

I watched Joseph stare out the window into the night. Every few minutes I tensed, preparing myself to lunge at him. I could take his eyes out, maybe, if I was fast. But even if I did, de Payens had that knife in his cane. And even if I had some plan for that, it would be too dangerous. Every time I talked myself into making a move—any move—I talked myself right out of it when I thought of the life growing inside me. I couldn't put our child in danger like that. Not until I knew it would be worth it.

There was no doubt in my mind that if I did nothing, de Payens would kill my child one way or another, and then kill me.

Reece was still alive, at least. But the connection between us seemed to be weaker now. If it was true that nothing but death could separate us then…

As I felt at the connection, it changed. Still weak, but there was a sudden surge of anger. My own heart sped up as adrenaline dripped into my own body in response to violence. As the rush faded, Reece was still there, and now more determined than ever. Alive. He'd gotten free.

"What are you smiling about?" Joseph asked.

He was watching me. I smoothed my expression to the best poker face I could manage. "Just comforting myself with all the ways I'm going to hurt the people that killed my mate," I said. "And anyone who threatens my baby."

Joseph looked me over slowly and snorted. "Yeah, okay."

Reece began to move closer. We were out of the desert now, on a highway. But he could tell where I was, and I could tell where he was—and he was coming for me. He was okay, and he was coming for me.

When he did, it would be swift vengeance. My mind raced with the possibilities of how it could play out. What would he do? Swoop down from the sky and burn the cars? No, he wouldn't risk me and our child. Stop us probably, then. Some way that was safer. But then de Payens would just hold me hostage again. So he was the one to watch when whatever it was happened. What would he do?

I played out every scenario I could imagine in my mind. Each time I did, a crippling nausea tried to overtake me.

"Looking a little pale," Joseph said.

"Don't antagonize him," de Payens murmured. "It's undignified. We aren't animals. Well." His eyes flicked toward Joseph. "Some of us aren't, in any case."

Joseph's jaw muscle twitched. He balled one hand into a fist, but went back to looking out the window.

He didn't like the Templars. Not any more than Reece did. It made me wonder why he'd struck the deal he did. I half hoped I would never know. That Reece would swoop down and kill them all, and take me away to somewhere remote where we could just live and raise our family and not be hunted.

It didn't feel like me. To imagine them all burning. Maybe it wasn't. Maybe it was Reece, pouring into me from far away.

It took two hours of thinking, waiting, watching, and worrying. When it happened, the only warning I got was a sudden, powerful sense of adrenaline and desperate concern. For me. I threw myself forward, and tore de Payen's cane from his hands as I dropped to the floorboard and curled around my stomach to protect my child.

Before de Payens could finish cursing, the Hummer lurched, tires screeched, and I slammed against his and Joseph's legs.

"Reece," de Payens spat. "Joseph. Deal with him. He shouldn't be able to shift, he'd already lost a pint of blood when we left."

Joseph grunted, and kicked his door open.

De Payens snarled down at me as Joseph left and raised his foot to stomp me. I didn't think, acting on instinct. I jerked the top of his cane free and jammed the blade that came with it into his leg.

He screamed as he snatched his leg away, and scrabbled to get a hand on the knife. With him distracted, I practically threw myself out the door Joseph had left through, and landed hard on the asphalt outside. De Payens was already coming through the door after me.

I clawed my way across the highway as I pushed to my feet and stumbled when a boot hit me hard in the ass, throwing me forward again. My arms wrapped around my stomach automatically, and my head slammed into the asphalt. Ringing filled my ears, and white spots flashed across my vision.

"Matthew!" It was Reece. His shout cut off with a grunt, and I saw multiples of Joseph tackling multiples of my mate.

"Reece!"

De Payens hauled me to my feet by my hair. I swung at him, but the strength had left my arms and all the rest of me and there was pounding, thunderous pain behind my eyes.

"I offered to do this the easy way," the Templar growled. "But if you'd rather die now, it's all the same to me. We've got the bones. We don't need you or your whelpling lizard. You were just a nice bonus."

He hauled the knife back.

No hand stepped in to stop him at the last moment. So I put my own hands between me and my belly. The metal bit into my palms as I closed my fingers around the blade and twisted it away, into de Payens' gut instead. I thrashed, throwing myself against the pommel to drive it deep.

De Payens let my hair go. I dropped, and stumbled away as he staggered back and grasped at the hilt of the knife. "You little whore…"

Grabbing the hilt only pained him more. He gasped in pain as one of his legs failed him and he dropped, still clawing at the knife to get it out as he crawled backward toward the car.

I turned in time to see Reece throw a haymaker punch. Joseph's head snapped to one side. He took a step back, and then another before he dropped. The Wolven hadn't hit the ground before Reece was moving in my direction. He paused only to see that de Payens was down, and then sprinted over the asphalt to me.

It was like I'd never been kissed before. Reece's lips crashed into mine, his arms encircling my shoulders as mine slipped around his waist. We were both breathless, heaving with the exertion of the fight. Grit scratched at our lips from the desert and the highway, and the scent of sweat filled my nostrils but I barely noticed anything except the points where our bodies touched again.

A thud of pain behind my eyes reminded me that I'd slammed my head into the ground. I winced, and Reece raised a hand to my cheek and sought out my eyes. "Are you injured? You fell. The baby?"

"I'm okay," I assured him. "I'm all right. I'm here. You made it. You came for me. Have you never turned on a television? What kind of dragon doesn't know what *dracarys* means? *Game of Thrones*? Mother of dragons? Burn the bitches?"

He laughed. "I haven't so much as looked at a working television since the forties, Matthew. It didn't seem that impressive. The years have passed quickly since then."

I groaned both from the pain and the amusement, and rested my head against his chest.

Behind me, de Payens coughed.

Reece's emotions grew hot. His expression turned to stone. "Mercy is in the car we arrived in. She's injured. You should join her. I will deal with de Payens."

"Reece, I—"

He put a finger to my lips. "It will be swift, and humane. But I cannot spare him. He will hunt us. Kill us, if he can. Go to Mercy. If not for her, I would not be here. We owe her our gratitude."

I knew he was right. Still, I turned to de Payens. "It didn't have to be this way."

The man spat. "Yes, it did. You'll see it. Eventually."

Reece put a hand on my lower back, and kissed the top of my head. "Go."

Survival. Fight or flight. It was me, and my baby, or this man. But Reece was right. I didn't have to see it. I'd seen enough that night. I turned and walked away, and made it about twenty feet before the sound of something breaking made me stop and shudder before I put my hands on my belly and walked on.

If de Payens meant what he'd said, something told me that it wouldn't be the last time I heard that sound.

Chapter 30
Reece

We returned to Catarina. Going back to the dig sight seemed untenable—the bones had been removed, Matthew explained, and Mercy required aid as quickly as possible. The local doctor accepted Mercy's explanation that she'd been mishandling a gun with quiet, patronizing patience. Our options for somewhere to stay were limited, of course, to the Tropic Inn and Suites.

Incredibly, the man behind the counter there was not only the same person as before—but I again detected the same sounds of moaning human females coming through his headphones as he pulled them off his ears to hang around his neck and check us in. If he recognized either Matthew or myself, he did not say so. He gave no comment to Mercy's bandaged arm either, and only went back to his pornography when we left him.

Mercy paused at the door to her room. "You two… aren't going to leave without me, right?"

"No," Matthew told her. He pulled her into a loose embrace, careful of her arm. "You're my doula, aren't you? How the hell am I supposed to have a baby without you?"

"Rest well," I wished her. "You have my deepest and undying gratitude, Mercy. We would not be here if it weren't for your cleverness."

She grinned wide, and stood a bit straighter. "Yeah. I guess that's true. I just hope it's not bad karma to hit a bad guy with a big rock."

It was hard to tell if she was joking or not. She disappeared into her room, and Matthew and I retired to the door across from hers.

"I'll be honest," Matthew said as we lumbered into our room, "I didn't miss this place and had hoped to never come back here ever again."

"We'll only be here briefly," I assured him. "There's someone coming down from the north. An outcast who may know more about how your pregnancy will play out, and the birthing process. An old dragon with a great deal of wisdom. I hope."

Matthew nodded, and slumped onto the bed. He put a hand to his head and winced.

Some of his pain was evident through our bond. I went to him, and placed my hands on his head where the road had scraped it. I passed some of my fire along both my touch and our bond, and was pleased when Matthew gave a quiet sigh of relief. He took my hand away and looked up at me. "You've got a big bag of tricks."

"We share my fire now," I told him. "As it heals me quickly, so does it heal you. Among other things."

"Do I get to grow wings and fly?" he asked.

"I'm afraid that is not among the benefits," I said. "Truthfully, I do not know their full extent. I can only feel it in you. I suppose we shall have to discover them together."

"You and me," he murmured.

"And our child," I agreed. "Our family."

He took a shaky breath. "Um… de Payens, when he had me… he said some things, Reece. I don't believe them—everything he said was a lie, I'm pretty sure—but I can't really help that I'm not sure I really know who you are. Not you, I mean—I'm certain about who *you* are. But your people. Their history. Their history with us…"

"He told you that we are predators," I guessed, "and that we once pillaged and violated humankind."

Matthew's lips thinned, and he nodded.

There was no sense in lying to him. My people did not have a clean history. "It was long before my time, and that of my generation," I said, holding his hand in mine but not so tightly that he could not withdraw, if that was his choice. "But there was a time when we were… more savage. Peace was made, eventually. I do not know the details well—only the ancients do—but my understanding is that our numbers dwindled in this world. We aged more quickly. The magic here is thin, not enough to sustain us indefinitely. But we did make peace."

"I believe you," Matthew whispered. "I do. And I've chosen my side in any case. I'm with you. My mate."

"And I with you," I swore. "You will never again leave my sight. I promise."

"My very own guardian dragon," he mused. "I kind of like that. Mmm… we're both pretty dirty. I should take a shower."

"Of course," I agreed.

He grinned. "After… I'm gonna need you to do the thing. You know the one."

We showered together, after that. I took my time, washing Matthew's wounds that were thankfully already beginning to heal, albeit slowly, and they were not extensive. Even after, I explored his body with both hands, spreading soap until he was slick all over, and our bodies glided like silk against one another, our cocks hardening and sliding between us until it was all I could do not to turn him around and knot him there and then.

His hand slipped between our stomachs and found my cock, slick with soap as he gripped me tight and stroked me slow, his lips brushing mine, our tongues flicking out to exchange passing caresses as my breath came more quickly and he gave teasing, quiet chuckles of delight each time my knees shook or my breath caught in my throat.

"I'm thinking we shouldn't get stuck in the shower," he said as his fingers found and caressed the skin at the base of me, where my knot swelled slightly at his touch and made me shiver.

"Agreed," I rasped. "Rinse."

We let the water cleanse us of soap, and when it was done we didn't bother drying off. I bent and hooked an arm under Matthew's knees, and scooped him up to my chest, nuzzling his nose with mine for a moment as the need to join with him again grew stronger. Navigating the narrow door was a puzzle, but at length I laid him out on the hard bed, and slid onto it next to him.

He rolled to his stomach at my gentle insistence, and spread his legs. I crawled behind him, and trailed kisses and fire down his spine, savoring the sounds he made for me. Matthew writhed under my treatment, the muscles along his back bunched and spasming as each bit of pleasure sparked and traveled over his skin and along nerves that echoed back to my own body. The anticipation in him swelled like a storm, and he gave a soft, plaintive whimper that made my knot flare—the same sounds he made when I was inside him. All my senses told me how ready he was, and it made my heart swell to feel how deeply he wanted me inside him. This was what having a mate truly meant then. Two halves a whole that ached to be reunited.

I reached the cleft of his smooth cheeks and parted them, and with delicate care bent and flicked my tongue across the pucker there. It twitched, clenching in reaction, but parted easily for me when I slipped the tip of my tongue into him and wriggled it there both to prepare him and to enjoy the way he came alive beneath me. His hips rocked and swayed, lifting off the bed to meet me, and he reached back to claw at my scalp with desperate, begging fingers.

A low growl left me and passed into him, sending vibrations that I now more fully understood thrumming into him. Matthew gave a choked cry, and I growled again as I pushed deeper, until I felt his opening yield to me. Inviting me in. In a moment, I was on his back, one hand milking slick fluid from my cock and onto his waiting ring. I used the thick head to smear it around, and gave myself two strokes to made myself wet enough before I eased forward.

Pure, sweet pleasure greeted me, and I let myself drown in the electric sea of Matthew's sensations as he pressed urgently against me, impatient to be filled. The brief pain that he felt was shared by both of us, but his hands and his hips told me that he did not want me patient, but hungry for him.

I thrust into him as deep as I was able, swallowed up by his body and a twinned fire that consumed us both.

"Reece," Matthew mewled, "fuck, baby... yes. Yes, I missed you so much. I love you."

My arms shook and wouldn't hold me, so I lowered myself onto him, reassured of his pleasure by the sudden swell of need that overtook him and flooded into me. I nipped at his earlobe as I withdrew and drove into him again, slow enough to give special care to the hard little gland inside him that made his body tremble. "I'll never leave you again," I promised. "I love you, Matthew. My mate. Mine forever. Yours forever."

He clenched around me, and met my next thrust as if he meant to throw me off. And then the next, and the next, urging me faster. My knot swelled gradually, popping in and out of his ring, grinding against his gland, and each time he howled my name.

"Harder," he wailed, "Reece please, fuck me deep... get me... make me... fuck, Reece, I'm almost there, make me come for you, *please*..."

It was all I could do to force myself inside the last thrust, my knot so swollen that I felt Matthew's brief flash of pain tinged with panic—it vanished when I pushed through and felt his hole close around the base of me. His gland swelled in response, and I bucked against him to massage it harder even as my own cock grew painfully hard and the fire of release ignited in my balls.

I bit down on his neck the moment that I spilled the first blinding shot of seed into him. In response, Matthew crowed desperation. His tunnel convulsed around my cock, milking the next two shots from me as he clamped down around my sensitive knot and the pulsed rhythmically as he came with me. I hold tight to him, and continued to buck, rubbing his gland and my knot together as we melted into a single, throbbing mote of orgasm that thundered through us both in waves that first overtook us entirely, reducing our thoughts and emotions to their primal components. Those waves passed, and were replaced with a soft, gentle current that should have made us glow like small stars.

We rolled together onto our sides, knotted tightly and sharing the little aftershocks between us as I nuzzled against the back of Matthew's head, and he threaded his fingers into mine and clasped them against his belly.

"Where will we go?" he asked after a time, when we'd drifted and woken, and drifted again.

I kissed his hair and his ear. "Somewhere remote," I mused. "Some small town where we can blend in, perhaps. Have our child in private. The outcasts know of many such places. They have to. They'll aid us. We will be safe."

He sighed contentedly, and wiggled tighter against me, as if it were somehow possible, and in time his breathing evened, and deepened, and he slept.

In the morning, when my knot had abated and I was able to withdraw, Matthew tended his business in the lavatory, and we showered together again. As we toweled off this time, despite a powerful desire to make love again, there was an urgent knock at the door.

Matthew's eyes widened. He looked to me, and then stepped into the bathtub again and squatted down in it, eyeing the curtain rod as, perhaps, a potential weapon.

I tied the towel around my waist and crept out to the door to peer through the small hole in it. When I saw the face on the other side, it was with a mix of relief and dread.

I opened the door, and stepped aside. "Yuri. Welcome."

The slender young man came into the room like a storm. "Matthew is with you? Why are you here? I meet your friend Mercy at breakfast in lobby, she was *shot*. Matthew?"

"I'm here," Matthew said quickly as he fastened his towel around his waist and emerged from the lavatory. "It's okay, Yuri. I'm okay."

Yuri charged Matthew with such speed that I nearly moved to get between them by instinct. I'm not sure I would have been fast enough. The two friends collided, and Yuri held Matthew tightly for long moments as he rattled off something in, I believe, Ukrainian.

When he'd had his fill, he held Matthew out at arm's length. "What has happened to you? Why would you let me think the worst? Do you have any idea what worry you caused me?"

I stood by quietly, wondering if Yuri realized that I was still in the room, or that Matthew and I were each clothed only in our towels. I closed the door quietly.

"Yuri," Matthew said, "I... I'm sorry. It's been an insane few months. Ah..."

He looked to me.

I could not deny my mate his human connections. It was clear, from his pleading eyes, that Yuri was someone he needed. I nodded once in answer to a silent question. We were on our own, after all, and there was some safety in numbers.

Matthew licked his lips, and waved at the bed. "You had, ah... you'd better sit down for this. It's kind of a long story."

Epilogue
Matthew

The year that followed was... not what I envisioned for myself before I left Portland.

Two of Reece's friends, Tarin and Sasha, also dragons, met us just north of Catarina. At Tarin's recommendation, we caravanned it east, ultimately to a town called Comfort. Small enough that any newcomers would be obvious, big enough to blend in after we'd been there a while.

Reece still had access to the dragons' hoard, which was good. We paid cash for a small ranch with a big house and a few smaller ones as well. And plenty of room for more, if we needed it.

"Place is far enough away from any claimed territory we shouldn't have an issue," Tarin explained. "And no Wolven packs nearby either. It's as safe as we can get, and we can always make it safer."

Sasha approved as well. But for very different reasons. "There's more like you in the world," he told me one night over dinner, the six of us gathered around a table. "We should be finding them. The Templars certainly are, and as soon as the first elder hears of it, and sues for dispensation from the ancients, our people will be looking, too."

"You want to bring them here?" I asked.

Sasha nodded, and was joined by Tarin and, ultimately, by Reece. "It would be prudent," Reece said. "If, indeed, there are more. They won't be safe on their own for long."

So it was decided. As for Yuri...

Yuri took everything with remarkable stride, though he remained skeptical until my belly finally started to swell in earnest. I would have loved to get an ultrasound and see the baby growing in stages but, well—explaining everything to the OB would have been difficult.

Mercy was a miracle. She hunted down textbooks and spent the year learning everything she could about midwifery, and needled Sasha endlessly about the vagaries of birth among sacred omegas. More than once, Sasha requested that we not tell her that he was skipping off to the north end of the ranch to get some quiet time.

The days and weeks ticked by, and then months. Mercy and Yuri seemed to enjoy taking turns making sure I was taking vitamins, eating enough, that I didn't forget to lotion the vast gourd that my abdomen had become. True to his word, Reece was never beyond shouting distance, and usually not beyond whispering distance.

Eventually, the day came.

It was a lot like being kicked in the stomach by a horse, about once every thirty minutes, but quickly picking up the pace until I was certain that whatever was happening, it was happening *wrong*.

Sasha had warned me how it would work, but had been utterly unable to convey just *how much* it would hurt. Reece held me against his chest as I pushed, and Mercy—bless her—played both coach and catcher while Yuri and the other dragons paced outside the small room that Mercy had insisted on decorating with all manner of crystals. There was soothing music, ostensibly, as well but I couldn't hear it over my own screaming.

It took nine hours, and a lot of swearing.

But in the end, Mercy finally gave a reverent gasp of delight and with tears in her eyes passed our child into my arms.

Not our son.

Our daughter.

"She's perfect," I gasped, as her blue eyes gazed lazily up at me. Her copper hair was matted against her head, and there was a lot of it. "Reece, look. We have a daughter. We made… we made a baby girl. Look at her…"

I looked up to see Reece's eyes wide and, for the first time, wet with tears. "A daughter. A… female dragon… she's the first in…"

He couldn't finish. Instead, he nuzzled close to us, his fire flooding me with warmth that I thought may have passed to her as well. Mercy left us alone.

"She needs a name," I said. "None of the ones we talked about will fit now."

"Sasha should name her," Reece said. "He's the oldest among us, and the eldest—"

I rolled my eyes and nudged him with my forehead to shut him up. "Sasha is a good man, and a good dragon, but I'm not letting him name our daughter. What about Danaerys?"

"Absolutely not," he chuckled. "No… but I do like Danni. What do you think?"

"Danni," I murmured, testing it on my tongue, the way it felt to croon it at her. "Little Danni the dragon."

"It's not a proper dragon name," Reece admitted, "but… perhaps it's time for new traditions. New ways. If I'd hewed the old, she wouldn't be in the world now. Our daughter is something new, Matthew. Something special."

"Yes, she is," I agreed. "Danni it is, then."

I curled her close, cradling her close. "Hello, Danni. I'm your daddy. And this is your papa. Don't tell anyone—but he's a *dragon*."

Reece had turned my life upside down. The day he saved me, everything changed. I knew, looking down at our daughter, that everything had just changed again. Not just for us, but for everyone. For the world, somehow, though I wasn't sure yet what it meant. But this time there was no fear.

This time, we would be ready. Together.

Printed in Great Britain
by Amazon